THE DELUSIONIST

Grant Buday

THE DELUSIONIST

ANVIL PRESS | VANCOUVER | 2014

Anvil Press Publishers Inc.
P.O. Box 3008, Main Post Office
Vancouver, B.C. V6B 3X5 CANADA
www.anvilpress.com

LIBRARY AND ARCHIVES CANADA CATALOGUING IN PUBLICATION

Buday, Grant, 1956-, author
          The delusionist / Grant Buday.

ISBN 978-1-927380-93-2 (pbk.)

          I. Title.

PS8553.U444D44 2014   C813'.54   C2014-900724-8

Printed and bound in Canada
Cover design by Rayola Graphic Design
Cover Illustration by Lauren Simkin Berke
Interior by HeimatHouse
Represented in Canada by the Publishers Group Canada
Distributed by Raincoast Books

The publisher gratefully acknowledges the financial assistance of the Canada
Council for the Arts, the Canada Book Fund, and the Province of British
Columbia through the BC Arts Council and the Book Publishing Tax Credit.

And the soul is up on the roof
in her night dress, straddling the ridge,
singing a song about the wildness of the sea
until the first rip of pink appears in the sky.
Then, they all will return to the sleeping body
the way a flock of birds settles back into a tree.

— BILLY COLLINS

PART ONE – 1962

In Which Cyril Meets His Match

ONE

OVER THE PAST MONTH Cyril and Connie had started to notice each other. It began in art class when everyone had to draw each other's mouth. Cyril did Connie's whole face. It was a good likeness, an uncanny likeness, right down to the sardonic narrowing of her already narrow eyes, the curl at the corner of her lips, and the nostrils alert to the scent of Cyril's excitement. Cyril knew he'd hit that one, like a ball square off the bat; the lines were not sketchy but bold, and even had flair. Sometimes it was like that: you lucked out, as if your hand did the work and you were just along for the ride. Not that Cyril admitted that to Connie.

"No putting pins in it," she said.

"Then you better be nice."

Her eyebrows rose in pleasant surprise as if discovering a worthy opponent while Cyril, breathless, went off to draw the next kid's mouth, feeling the exhilarating heat of Connie Chow's attention. Connie was strange. She once came to school with her teeth blacked out, another time wearing a boot and a runner, and once wearing a shiny red clown's nose. She always used one of those painted Chinese umbrellas. Some said she was from *The Twilight Zone*. When she walked by they whispered just loud enough to be heard, *"Picture if you will an alien who looks almost human…"* She was an object of fear and disdain—disdain because she was small and skinny, fear because she was confident and unpredictable. The very elusiveness of her approval made it all that much more desirable to Cyril, who wanted it, meaning he wanted her. Somehow she managed to be terrifying and reassuring at the same time, and while she might say no thanks if he asked her out he knew she wouldn't sneer, so he decided to do it right after school.

Art was the last class of the day. Cyril lingered on the steps trying to appear casual even as his mind was fizzing like a shaken Pepsi. He debated whether to sit or stand, and if he stood what sort of pose to take, hands in or out of his pockets, and if he did put his hands in his pockets should it be his front pockets or back pockets? But if he had them in the back it might look as if he was scratching his butt. And yet if they were in the front ones it might look even worse, as if he was playing pocket pool. Maybe if he hooked his thumbs over his belt? Yes, he could hook his thumbs over his belt, cool, like Gary Cooper. Except he wasn't wearing a belt. He considered standing with his arms crossed but that would look like impatience. He groaned. All he wanted was to ask her to go see *The Apartment* with Jack Lemon. He rehearsed it in his mind. *So. Connie.* Too abrupt? *Connie, hi, I was kind of wondering if maybe…* Too passive? *Hey, Connie, I'm going to see The Apartment. Interested?*

In the midst of this rehearsal she appeared, book bag thumping like a dead dog at the end of a leash as she descended the steps.

He turned toward her, nearly snagging his right toe on his left heel, his words stumbling out faster than intended. "Connie hey hi how you doing?"

She halted on the step above him which put them eye to eye. She was tiny, about five-one, wore a tartan skirt and a jean jacket with the collar turned up. Her bangs touched her eyebrows making her hair resemble a helmet, and she was chewing a big wad of Black Cat bubble gum. "Okay."

He had hoped for something more substantial, a springboard for further conversation, a delightful discovery of shared interests. "Yeah?"

She shrugged. She chewed with her mouth open then blew a bubble that popped over her lips and she chewed it back in as if gathering a black parachute into her mouth. "How about you, Cyril? You okay?"

"Good. You know. Fine."

"Glad to hear it." Her bemused tone reminded him that they'd seen each other only minutes ago. Kids streamed by whooping at their freedom, punching each other, or slouching off to hack a butt. Connie watched them pass with lidded eyes. Was she getting bored standing there with him? She blew another bubble, smaller this time, which popped with a snap. He could smell the faintly liquorice scent of the gum.

"Wanna go see *Psycho*?" He nearly choked. What was he doing? What had possessed him? *The Apartment* was safe and funny; *Psycho* was weird and horrific.

She stopped chewing. "You do realize it's restricted."

Of course he realized it was restricted. He was seventeen; you had to be twenty-one. But it was too late to turn back, so he shrugged offhandedly as if he went to restricted movies all the time. He saw her gauging that shrug, measuring it. As he awaited her answer, his pulse thumped a countdown in his skull: three...two...one...

"Sure."

"Great."

And with that she hoisted her book bag, black canvas with a red drawstring, onto her shoulder and proceeded on down the steps. At the street she turned and looked at him, head tilted appraisingly, and waved as though wiping mist from a window.

All week Cyril was in a panic. He recalled paying a quarter to inhale a chest full of helium at the PNE, an experience simultaneously exhilarating and slightly sickening. Each time he and Connie met in the hallway or the cafeteria they nodded or, it seemed to him, purposely pretended not to see each other, as if they had an unspoken agreement. Was this a sign of an intuitive connection or a sign that they—she—was having second thoughts? He couldn't imagine Connie Chow nervous. She'd been in the school performance of *A Midsummer Night's Dream* as Helena, and while the other kids over-acted or stood like mannequins, she made you believe. Cyril had watched understanding that she was exposing herself, taking the risk of humiliation with the entire school watching, and that therein lay her strength.

Friday afternoon she appeared in the hallway, book bag slung over her shoulder as if she was a hobo hitting the road. "So, meet you out front of the theatre, okay."

Cyril nodded quickly, relieved at the casualness though at the same time a little disappointed. Shouldn't they be going to the theatre together? Wasn't he supposed to knock on her door? Or were they just buddies? He hadn't been pals with a girl since he was five years old.

Saturday his anxiety mounted. His mother saw something was up.

"Vut?"

"*What*, not *vut*."

She grew defiant. "*Vut*."

His mother's accent was a blunt and plaintive lament, embedded with centuries of history: eras of glory and eras of defeat, cathedrals and palaces built, cathedrals and palaces burned. Cyril habitually measured his own speech against her accent, fearing that it would erupt through his own perfectly pitched English, the way his voice had occasionally betrayed him during puberty. "Nothing."

They were in the kitchen watching the funeral across the alley. She turned from the dark pageant and regarded her son. She was not a big woman yet bore an aura of weight, as though gravity reserved a special force for her alone. "You're pacing."

"I'm not pacing."

"Here—there. You'll wear out the floor. You need to pee go pee."

His mother had dyed black hair wound in a braid around her head. When Cyril was small he liked to touch it because it felt like thick silk rope. Sometimes she had a bun on top, sometimes at the back, and sometimes one at either side, but it always involved some kind of braid. She had high, broad cheekbones, a thin nose, a small mouth, and favoured heavy red lipstick and skirts of bright yellow or robin's egg blue.

"If I needed to pee I'd pee."

She responded with an elaborate shrug. It was two in the afternoon and she was still in her housecoat, faded yellow flowers on a faded blue background, and wore feathered slippers which made it look as though she had hens on her feet. She was on her third pot of Darjeeling. On the table sat a loaf of rye bread, a plate of sliced ham, some garlic sausage, some dill pickles. She pointed to the funeral procession with her thumb—one hearse, half a dozen people, no flowers—and nodded with grim satisfaction. "Only a man could have such a small funeral. A bachelor. Or—" And here she became worldly in a way Cyril did not want to consider. "If it's a woman she was a slut." She pursed her lips up under her nose and sniffed dismissively as if she'd seen it before and knew of what she spoke. "You must be shit on a shoe for such a small funeral."

Cyril couldn't bear another one of her "Lives of the Deceased," based on the scale of the funeral, the quality of the coffin, and the number of bouquets, so escaped out the back door to the carport. The oil stain on the concrete used to be the shape of Ukraine; now it was nothing, smoke, a ghost, not of the land his parents and brother had escaped, but of the car they used to own, a Nash Rambler convertible with white-walled tires. Cyril's dad had loved that car, loved its name and all that it implied, as if it was the very epitome of life in the new world, or, as his dad would have put it: *noo vorld*. When he died it sat dripping oil in the carport for a year and then, just when his mother decided to get her license, it was stolen.

Cyril leaned against the wall and watched the hearse beyond

the hedge. It was a sunny May morning, swallows skimming the grass, bees in his mother's roses. She had a grudging admiration for roses: feed them shit and they bloomed bright and radiant and smelling of perfume. He slid down the wall and sat with his knees up, the voice of the priest reaching him from the grave, and wondered how it was possible to look forward to something and dread it at the same time.

That evening he waited outside the theatre. Downtown Granville Street was all neon marquees: the Coronet, the Orpheum, the Plaza, the Caprice, the Lyric. The line-up for *Psycho* ran halfway down the block. Hands in his pockets he tried to appear casual, reminding himself that he wasn't some schmuck alone on a Saturday night, he had a date. The evening was warm and the crowd eager. He'd shaved what little he had to shave, first with the grain and then against it, then looked at his clothes wondering what to wear. His church suit? He hadn't been to church in two years, and discovered that the sleeves of the jacket ended mid-forearm and the pants mid-shin. He opted for clean jeans and a white T-shirt and his black Converse All Stars. Standing before the bathroom mirror he gauged his chances of passing for twenty-one. It didn't look good. He toyed with the idea of sketching a moustache on his upper lip and a pair of sideburns. What if he was taller? He was five-foot-eight, so maybe another inch would do the trick. Taking a thick stack of pages from one of his sketch pads he traced his feet and cut them out making insoles which he fit into his runners. It felt different but he didn't see much extra height, and by the time he'd walked all the way downtown to the theatre—too nervous to sit fidgeting on the bus—he'd packed the paper insoles flat.

"Hey."

He stared.

Connie had painted her eyelids gold, put on thick red lipstick, a black and red Suzie Wong dress with a high collar, and spike heels that made her the same height as Cyril. She'd also suddenly sprouted breasts—nice ones. She slid her arm inside Cyril's and they strolled to the end of the line. He felt terror, pride, and a painfully rigid erection. The line began to move.

"Someday I'm gonna be in movies," she said as though stating her intention of going into dentistry.

Cyril didn't doubt it for a minute. She was focused and she had talent. What was he going to do? His dad had been a welder, his brother Paul was studying to be an accountant, and his own sole talent was drawing, which left courtroom sketches, police profiles, or sitting in Stanley Park on Sundays doing two-dollar portraits.

At the ticket window Connie stepped ahead of him and in a tone of absolute confidence said, "One, please."

The ticket seller was a pale and balding man in a white shirt and black bow tie. A cigarette smouldered in the ashtray by his elbow and the fumes filled the booth and seeped like fog through the hole where you slid your money. He studied her, hesitated, then like some gate keeper in a fairy tale succumbing to a spell, he smiled and pushed a ticket through the smoke.

"Thank you."

"Enjoy the show."

"If I don't I will most certainly expect you to refund my money."

The ticket seller seemed to enjoy that. Connie was through,

she'd made it. Cyril's gut sickened. When he stepped up the clerk exhaled and smoke blasted like dragon fire through the hole in the window. "Got ID?"

Cyril put one hand on his hip and managed a sarcastic smirk, all the while horribly aware of everyone behind him. He tried sounding amused. "What?"

The clerk tapped the black panther sticker on the window. "Gotta be twenty-one. You twenty-one?"

Connie already had her ticket torn in two and was waiting, arms crossed, eyebrows elevated, as if growing impatient. Only bold action could save him. "Twenty-one? I'm twenty-*two*."

"Yeah?" The clerk considered that. "Wish I was still twenty-two. Can you prove it?"

Cyril's face burned and he desperately needed a toilet.

The man was not unsympathetic. "Nice try, kid." He motioned Cyril aside and the next person stepped up.

"*Swiss Family Robinson*'s down the street," called some wag, earning a big laugh.

◦◦ ◦◦

When *Psycho* let out the women in the crowd were clinging to the arms of their escorts. There was Connie. She rolled her shoulders provocatively causing her new breasts to rise and fall. Cyril tried not to stare, but one of those breasts was now riding distinctly lower than the other. She took his arm, leaned close and glanced fearfully around. "It was so freaky." Cyril smelled the buttered popcorn on her breath and saw that her lips were shiny. "I think I clawed the padding off the arm of the seat." Cyril's own arm ached in envy of that seat. She must have seen the expression on his face. "You got to look the look, man. Play the part. *Be* the part. What did you get up to?"

He considered saying he went for a beer except the BS wasn't working too well for him this evening. "Walked."

"And what did you see as you walked?"

He traced the horizon with an open palm. "The city."

"In all its magnificence?"

"Its heights and depths. Its dreams and despairs. While you sat, I voyaged."

"I'm jealous." She leaned against him and in spite of everything Cyril was suddenly happy walking along Granville with her, even if he was also a little indignant that she hadn't cashed in her ticket. After all there would have still been time to catch *The Apartment*. They got on the bus and sat at the back. Connie unbuttoned her high-necked dress and reached inside her brassiere and pulled out an orange.

"I'm starved." She pulled out the other one and offered it.

Cyril felt the bus pitch like a small boat in a steep sea. She set the warm fruit in his cold hand: its heat penetrated his palm. No ball of gold, no meteor, no bauble from an ancient treasure hoard was more valuable. As the bus wheezed and jolted up Granville they peeled and ate their oranges—the sweetest orange he'd ever experienced. At Forty-First Avenue they transferred and headed east then got off and walked, the lines in the sidewalk ticking past beneath their feet as if they were walking railroad racks. Cyril's mind raced ahead. Kiss her? Ask her out again? When they reached her gate she took care of all questions by hanging her arms over his shoulders and kissing him, not a peck but a real kiss, long and lingering; sighing she moved closer.

"I loved your drawings," she whispered. "I could taste the metal, like blood in my mouth."

He was alarmed, and yet apparently she liked that. "I'm glad."

"It was real," she said, her tone implying she was starved for something real.

Cyril had two drawings in the year-end show. One was of his dad's hammer and pliers and welding mask. The other was of a small anvil with an egg balanced on top. Both drawings were done in pencil that shone like dully gleaming lead, and both were big, two-by-three feet, and filled the paper to the edges. He'd worked for weeks on them down in the basement at his dad's old workbench.

Cyril and Connie kissed some more and all the way home he tasted citrus.

∽ ∾

The next afternoon he and Gilbert tossed the football in the alley. Gilbert dropped back and launched a bomb. "Kapp!" he shouted. Cyril sprinted. "Willie the Wisp!" Gilbert's throw sailed over the hedge and into the cemetery and struck a gravestone and went wobbling off across the grass. Shoving his way through the laurel hedge Cyril retrieved it. Gilbert's every second throw bounced off carport roofs, flattened flowers, or shattered graveyard vases. But he hurled the ball with a gusto Joe Kapp would have envied.

Later, they headed for their booth in the Aristocratic, where Gilbert set his elbows on the table and leaned forward demanding details.

Cyril knew a kiss wouldn't count for Gilbert nor would an orange, no matter where it had been, so he shrugged and tried to appear offhand.

"Not even a feel?"

Cyril tasted citrus again, but how could he mention that?

"Figures." Gilbert sat back, relieved that Cyril hadn't jumped ahead in the race to losing their virginity. "What did you see?"

"*Psycho.*"

"Sure, and I got two cocks."

Cyril said nothing, merely gazed off out the window at the traffic. Silence was the only weapon that worked with Gilbert; you had to wait him out.

"No shit?"

"You don't really see anything," he said, hoping Connie would cover for him.

Gilbert yawned as if it didn't matter anyway. He had a dismissive manner, as if he'd heard everything before. He had long teeth, dark blue eyes, and hair as thick and black as a slab of fresh tar. His jaw was big but his nose small, as if his features had been mismatched.

"I'm thinking of killing myself," said Gilbert. They'd known each other since the first grade, long enough for Cyril to indulge such posturing. Gilbert had no intention of croaking before he made his million. He was obsessed with schemes that ranged from forgery—using Cyril's draughting skills—to robbing Shaughnessy mansions, to stealing whisky from Seagrams where his old man drove a forklift. Not a huge money-maker, that last one, but it would give him 'operating capital.'

Cyril indulged him. "You down?"

"Bored."

"Who isn't?" Cyril watched the cars waiting at the intersection. When the light changed they began moving forward in an obedient fashion, as if they were all hypnotized, obeying some voice from above. Was that the future? Was that adulthood? Cyril worried about the future, but he wasn't the least bit bored, not now, not since his date with Connie.

"How you going to do it?"

"Dunno."

"Poison?"

Gilbert grimaced. "I wanna die, not suffer."

"Carbon monoxide?"

"The old man won't even let me start the car."

"Booze and pills?"

"Blow it and they put you in Riverview and you end up wearing pyjamas the rest of your life."

"Shoot yourself."

"Kind of requires a gun."

"Drown?"

Now Gilbert sat forward. "That might be good. Lemme borrow your weight shoes."

His weight shoes were new: cast iron, Joe Weider, and had cost him eight bucks. "Buy your own."

"You'll get them back when they drag the bottom."

"Put rocks in your pockets."

"It's my last request."

"What if they don't find you?"

"I'll leave a note and a map."

"I'll think about it."

The next Saturday Cyril and Connie saw *The Apartment*, and they held hands and afterward walked across the bridge then angled their way home, eventually reaching the corner of the cemetery. Connie said she envied him living across from a graveyard. Cyril went into a Bela Lugosi accent. "Ze smell of ze cemetery is good. It remind me of Transylwania."

"The veeping and moaningk is music to my pointed ears," she said, right on cue.

They wandered around reading headstones by starlight. Many graves had photos set right into the markers. Connie bent to read something scratched into a slab: "*Bastard. I'm glad you're dead.*" She gave a thumbs up. "Nice."

It was a warm night and they heard cars beating their way up Fraser Street. Sharing a piece of *Black Cat* gum, they stood face-to-face and blew bubbles that touched and popped over each other's mouths and then chewed them from each other's lips. He hooked his forefinger into the front pocket of her jeans and she did the same to his and they stood there, both leaning away and holding each other's weight in a game of trust, then they pulled toward each other and kissed again.

"We taste good," she said.

He embraced her and slid one hand down to her rear. She removed the hand but held on to it and they resumed walking through the trees. Connie patted the trunk of a maple as though it was the haunch of a horse.

This was his favourite tree in all the graveyard. He'd spent a lot of time in that tree, contemplating life and death, the past and the future, the North Shore Mountains, and the crows that migrated east each evening. How appropriate—how right—that it was the one Connie chose to pat.

Connie reached for the lowest branch but it was too high, so Cyril made a stirrup of his hands and hoisted her up. She caught the limb and hung there a moment, feet pedaling the air before hauling herself into a sitting position against the trunk.

"Okay, see you," chirped Cyril.

"Fine. I'll become a tree spirit. Every autumn when my leaves fall you'll hear my lament in the wind." She put the back of her wrist to her brow.

He leapt and pulled himself up beside her. The world smelled of grass and sap and bark and Black Cat gum. The next branch was within easy reach. They moved methodically from limb to limb and the higher they went the farther away school, the city, the world receded.

"Think we'd die if we fell?" she asked.

"Only if we landed on our heads." He thought he should suggest this to Gilbert.

"What if we only got brain damage and drooled all the time?"

"Here." Four branches fanned from one side of the trunk forming a platform. Cyril lay on his back with his hands behind his head. Through the leaves he saw stars.

Connie positioned herself beside him and they lay a long time without speaking, the only sounds the far-off traffic and the applause of the leaves stirring in the warm wind.

TWO

AS THEY SLID into a booth at the Aristocratic, Connie found a copy of the *Sun* and began paging through it. Her eyes goggled. "Cyril..."

By the stricken look on her face he thought someone must have died. "What?"

"They shut down Lenny Bruce last night at Isy's!" She threw herself back and seemed to have trouble breathing. Staring past the booth's juke box, she nodded with slow deliberation as if at one more piece of evidence and stated, "This is why I gotta get out of here."

Cyril had seen Lenny Bruce on the *Steve Allen Show*. Dirty comic. Sick comic. Drug addict. But he was funny. "Get out of here—when?" he asked as casually as possible.

"I don't know." She sat forward, elbows on the table, and as she reread the article she rubbed her temples as if in pain. "Soon."

It was the first he'd heard of this plan.

She folded the paper and slid it aside. "What a two-bit back woods town."

Cyril felt naive for never having had such a sophisticated thought. He was seated with his back to the door but he heard it open and saw Connie's eyes shift.

She leaned closer and said in a low voice, "Look at them."

Cyril turned and saw his brother with a girl a full head taller than him. When Paul spotted Cyril he winced as if at a sour smell and steered the girl to the farthest booth.

Connie asked, "What's with him?"

Cyril said, "He kind of hates me because I didn't have to eat leaves."

"So your family used to be cows?"

"In the war. They had to eat dandelions. Or shoes. Or both. I don't know. They boiled nails and drank the water for the iron. He thinks I pulled a fast one by not being born until after."

"Is that why he's a runt?"

Paul was five-foot-three, with bad teeth, brittle bones, and a pinched chin. "Maybe."

"My dad says in China they eat grasshoppers."

"Raw?"

She was indignant. "Baked. Or barbecued. With sauce."

"Does he tell you a lot about China?"

"He doesn't know anything about China except what he reads in *Reader's Digest*."

The discussion of Paul, China, and eating grasshoppers buried Connie's declaration about leaving Vancouver. Cyril hoped it was a performance, like Gilbert's suicide talk.

That evening at supper Paul said, "So who's the chow mein Lily you were all kissy-kissy with?"

"Who was that guy you were holding hands with?"

Paul lunged across the table but Cyril was too fast.

"Interracial marriage is illegal in some places, you know. You could be put in jail."

"So is homosexuality," said Cyril. "But at least you'd be with guys."

Paul sneered.

Cyril almost felt bad. It was awkward being bigger than his older brother. But Paul was always provoking him. So far there'd been no racial remarks at school, which was a relief because if there were Cyril knew he'd have to fight. But what a noble cause! Not that he and Connie made a big performance of kissing in the hallways or holding hands like some couples who liked turning their relationships into theatre. He went to the kitchen sink and began doing the dishes. He liked the hot water on his hands.

"Yeah, that's about your level. Get used to it. You'll be washing dishes the rest of your life."

Cyril tried to sound charmed, as if Paul had complimented him. "You think so?"

"I know so."

Yet he worried that Paul might be right. Art and Phys. Ed. were the only subjects he excelled in and Paul never let him forget it. "Dishwashing's a fine art," said Cyril. "You gotta have brains to be a dishwasher."

"Is that a fact?" Paul went downstairs to his bedroom and returned with a book. "Okay, genius. Let's find out how smart you are." He slapped a book down on the counter. *Test Your Own IQ*.

"I know how smart I am."

"Yeah, how smart? This smart?" Paul indicated an inch between his thumb and forefinger. "Or this smart?" Paul stretched his thumb and forefinger as wide as they'd go. Paul was wearing a black turtleneck sweater and black jeans and perfectly shaped sideburns. He was twenty-four and finishing up the CGA program at UBC. Seven years younger, Cyril was five inches taller and thirty pounds heavier. "Everyone wants to know how smart they are." Paul became soothing. "You're right. You're smart enough to be a dishwasher. You could probably be head dishwasher—if you worked hard," he added. He held the book out. Cyril considered punching Paul—not in the face but in the chest—just hard enough to drop him on his ass and maybe knock the wind out of him. Paul however beat him to the action by whacking him across the chest with the book. "Go on. It'll be fun."

"My hands are wet," said Cyril.

"I guess you haven't learned about tea towels yet," said Paul sympathetically. "That'll come next semester. See." He took one from the drawer and showed it to Cyril.

Cyril dried his hands.

"Go on," said Paul in the fond and encouraging tone of a mentor. He set the book in Cyril's hand. Cyril looked at it: light, small, seemingly innocent. He tossed the book into the soapy water, which splashed up onto the window and drooled down like saliva.

"Your honour," said Paul in his best Perry Mason, "I rest my case."

∽ ∾

Cyril and Connie spent the summer at the movies, at the beach, and in the cemetery. It was hot and dry and the cemetery grass grew pale and crisp and the rare breeze coursing through made the leaves shimmer.

One afternoon on the way to her house they discussed *The Hawaiian Eye*. Cyril said Nancy Kwan would be better as Cricket than Connie Stevens. "But you'd be better than either of them," he added. "You've got presence."

"Presence?" She sounded sceptical yet attentive.

"Star quality."

That was too much. "Oh fuck off you bullshitter you." But she couldn't contain her delight. How open and innocent and vulnerable her face looked.

"I'm serious." He gazed frankly into her eyes.

She turned away. It was not often that Connie couldn't meet his gaze. She seemed to be studying something in the distance, something she wanted, her eyes hopeful, her mouth slightly open. After a few moments she turned back to him and said, "Want to see my sword collection?"

It was the first time he'd been in her house. Would it be like a pagoda, with dragons and black lacquer furniture? From the outside it looked standard, an older place with wooden steps leading up to a deep porch with squared pillars and stained glass windows flanking the panelled door.

As soon as they entered the house they saw an elderly woman standing in the living room as though waiting for them. She looked nothing like the balding crones scuffing up and down the Chinatown sidewalks in baggy pants and matching coats lugging bags bulging with tumorous vegetables. She was slim and elegant and stood with her hands primly folded before her.

"Grandma, this is Cyril Androidchunk," said Connie.

"Enchantee." She held out a lily-like hand, pinky poised. It took Cyril a full half minute before he understood that he was supposed to kiss it. He did. It smelled of jasmine.

The living room had a Danish modern couch with matching chairs and coffee table, on the mantel ceramic black panthers and above it a gold landscape: gold lake, gold tree, a gold man and a gold woman in a gold pagoda. And Connie's grand-mother, her hands folded once again like a society hostess at a soirée.

"Bon après midi," she said.

"Bon après midi," replied Cyril. He put his hand on the newel post carved like a pineapple and went up the stairs after Connie.

"Thinks she's France Nuyen." Connie took a key ring from her pocket and gave it a jingle. "I like keys," she said. "And locks. Something about them."

"An answer and a question," said Cyril without thinking, and it occurred to him to draw locks and keys, that you could do a whole series of locks and keys.

This arrested her attention. She extended the key toward his chest and making a single click with her tongue gave the key a twist as if opening him up.

Connie entered her room. Cyril hesitated: he'd fantasized about her room: the look, the smell, the very air, convinced it must be a dimension beyond his most erotic visions, a boudoir of silks and oils and incense. The first thing he saw was himself in a full length mirror, the second thing was a sword at his neck.

"En garde, English pig dog." Connie's left hand gripped the

sword and her right perched on her hip. Her chin was high, her left knee bent. "Cool, eh." She lowered the blade and leaned on it like a cane.

Cyril felt his neck for blood. "Where'd you get that?"

"It's an épée." She sliced the air making the blade sing.

"It's dangerous."

"Elle est *très* dangerous," she corrected him.

On the wall half a dozen swords lay in a rack. Broad blade, narrow blade, curved blade, scimitar.

Connie stood before the mirror making faces at herself. Left eyebrow up, left eyebrow down. Right eyebrow up, right eyebrow down. Sad face. Happy face. She screamed silently, then let her head fall back and laughed silently. Finally she gave her cheeks a vigorous rub between her palms then clapped her hands together. "Come on." She slid the window up and climbed onto the roof. Cyril leaned on the sill and looked out and discovered that it was a long way down, with the jutting pickets of a fence waiting like fangs.

"Hey." She was straddling the ridge above him, wiggling her toes. Letting her head fall back she emitted a yowl like a newly escaped soul.

He groped his way up onto a roof mountainous with ridges and slopes, and found Connie lying in a valley and staring at the sky. He stretched out next to her, their shoulders touching, the asphalt shingles hot beneath their backs and the rest of the world far away.

She said, "The Big Bang happened but didn't happen anywhere, space was born with the Big Bang. Something can happen nowhere."

Cyril tried grasping that.

"We have to free ourselves from the restraints of three dimensional space."

Cyril stared into the boundless blue and felt his brain straining to comprehend the concept. *The restraints of three dimensional space...* He wondered if God set off the Big Bang the way he and Gilbert set off firecrackers at Halloween, for the hell of it, for the noise and the light and the plain old fun of seeing what would happen. Maybe God was a bored old guy looking for a diversion from the monotony of eternity. His hand was only inches from Connie's hip. What would happen if he put it on her thigh, or—and here the world reeled—undid her zipper? The very thought made his pants tighter. He slid his hand closer.

"Sometimes I come up here at night."

His hand crept closer still.

"I'd sleep up here but I sleepwalk."

He imagined her walking in her sleep, arms out like a zombie. "Do you wear pyjamas?"

"Cyril," she said, mock appalled. "Now and again. I suppose you're going to tell Gilbert."

"I don't tell Gilbert anything," he lied, even as he vowed never to tell him this. Then he told her how Gilbert was looking for a way to commit suicide.

She considered this a long time, which caused Cyril a spasm of angst thinking Connie might approve, that it might make Gilbert interesting. She said, "He asked me out last week."

It was as if the air had been sucked from his lungs. His fingertips clutched at the gritty shingles to keep from plunging off the roof into the sky.

She patted his knee. "Hey, don't worry. It's no contest. I said no." Then she added, "Maybe he could do a swan dive from his roof."

"Maybe I'll push him off," said Cyril, who was not at all shocked by Gilbert's betrayal. It wouldn't be the first time he'd tried stealing from him. They were best friends but they were competitive. Who was taller, who was stronger, who could spit further, piss longest. "Why does your grandmother want to be France Nuyen?"

"Because France Nuyen is beautiful and exotic."

∽ ∾

Cyril's mother said invite Connie to supper. He was wary. His mother hated Russians and Germans, and was sceptical of Austrians, Hungarians, Rumanians and Turks, and despised the Commies, so what did she think of the Chinese?

Connie expressed no reaction when she entered the Andrachuk's living room and saw a weeping Virgin the size of a garden gnome on the cabinet in the corner, the dozens of Virgin Marys on the mantel, the painting of the Madonna and Child, the Bibles and the candles, the Nativity scenes embroidered on the cushions. Seeing it through Connie's eyes it took on a strange and alien aspect, and Cyril found himself sniffing the air fearing it smelled of the cabbage his mother insisted on cooking. When his mother entered the room she halted at the sight of Connie, who was wearing a short-sleeved white blouse, pleated plaid skirt, flat-soled black shoes. Cyril waited fearfully. His mother's chin was elevated and her eyebrows up. She smiled and opened her arms and embraced Connie. Soon they were chatting like old friends, the weather, the neighbourhood, Connie's plans.

"Vould—*would*—you like tea?"

"I'd love tea."

"Cyril," she said, not looking at him. "Tea."

He retreated to the kitchen and made tea, returning a few minutes later to find his mother and Connie on the couch, knee-to-knee, holding hands. He set the tray on the table. The teapot was in the shape of a pumpkin with matching cups.

"Pour."

He poured.

"Ekting," she said, nodding as though it was an interesting concept. "You get job, ekting?"

"Ma."

She turned and considered Cyril. "What job you will get?"

"I'm fine."

She nodded, the corners of her mouth down, eyebrows up, as if to say that was an amusing opinion though as naive as every other idea in his head. She turned back to Connie. "He has no direction. His brother is CGA."

"CGA." Connie nodded as though, like *ekting*, that too was an interesting concept.

It was a Wednesday evening in August. Paul had moved out at the beginning of the summer yet still showed for supper three or four times a week. This turned out to be one of those evenings.

"Acting?" said Paul over the boiled potatoes and roast pork. "Acting like what?"

Cyril gripped his butter knife ready to stab him.

Connie regarded Paul with lidded eyes. "Like a queen, of course." And then, waiting just long enough for awkwardness to set in, she added, "Either that or I'll open a laundry."

No one breathed much less spoke. Then Connie laughed. Paul was so surprised his habitual sneer melted and he too laughed, long and loudly.

∽ ∾

They went to see *Gypsy*. Even in the privacy of the theatre's darkness Cyril tried not staring too hard at Natalie Wood's thighs and cleavage, yet he need not have worried because Connie was so rapt she forgot he was even there. They sat in the seventh row, her favourite row, the perfect row, just close enough but at the same time far enough away that your neck didn't kink. She sat deep in her seat, gripping the armrests, absorbing the silver screen's transcendent radiance. There was Natalie Wood in pink feathers squaring off against her mother, Rosalind Russell, clad in black. "Look at me, momma. Look at me. No education. From Seattle. Look at me now. I'm a star!"

Seattle, just down the road from Vancouver. Cyril remembered going to Seattle in the Nash Rambler, the top down, his dad's wrist draped over the wheel, his mother in sunglasses and a polka-dotted scarf, Paul happy watching the American countryside spinning past even if it was identical to that north of the border.

When the film ended they remained in their seats while the others moved in a slow herd up the aisles and lit cigarettes. Only when the theatre was empty and the lights came on did Connie seem to breathe again. She blinked and stood, slowly, and when she looked at Cyril he had the eerie sensation that she didn't recognize him.

"You okay?"

She didn't answer, she turned and headed up the aisle. They were out of the theatre and down the street when Cyril took her hand. She hadn't said a word since the lights had gone down at the start of the movie. "Hello."

She looked at him, and in a perfect Rosalind Russell—deep and sinewy—said, "I was born too soon and started too late."

It was uncanny: she *was* Rosalind Russell, taller, older, with a sweet and agonized scorn in her eyes. All the way home she riffed bits of dialogue. Not Wood's, but Russell's. Striding ahead she whirled to face Cyril. "You like it, well I got it." Clenching her fists at her sides she shook her chest. "How do you like these egg rolls!"

∽ ∾

The last Monday before school resumed they bussed to Kits Beach. Freighters filled the harbour and limp-sailed yachts sat on their own shadows. As they walked along the sand Connie brushed her palm against the back of Cyril's head feeling the bristles of his crewcut while he stroked her hair as though petting a mink. The beach was crowded but they found a secluded spot at the far end by a log, dropped their towels and plunged into the water. He caught her around the waist and lifted her high and they rolled and wrestled.

Baring her teeth like a shark she asked, "Would you eat human flesh?"

"Only if I didn't know whose it was."

"Yeah, that makes sense."

"And only a woman. This is a weird conversation."

"You think so?"

"Kind of. But I wouldn't mind taking a bite out of you."

She pretended to slap his face. He caught her hand and kissed it giving the palm a quick lick. She put her licked palm to his cheek then pinched his earlobe at which he caught her thumb between his teeth as if to take a bite. They swam to shore and waded out holding hands. She was wearing a backless one-piece displaying a surprisingly curvy figure. Her nipples stood as stiff as light switches beneath the sunflower yellow suit and Cyril desperately wanted to touch them. He quickly turned away and lay face down on his towel.

"Can you do my back?"

She was kneeling over him holding a tube of *Coppertone*. When she was on her stomach Cyril got up and poured the oil where her suit dipped to the small of her back. She moaned as he massaged it in, feeling the smooth surface of her skin, the bumps of her spine, the gentle ridges of her shoulder blades, the rise of her hips, and, within inches of his hand, her bum under the taut wet fabric and below that her parted thighs. He did the backs of her knees and her calves and stopped at the soles of her feet which were coated in sand. He envisioned sliding his fingers between her toes and then sucking them slowly one by one. He quickly put the cap back on the oil and lay down, his face turned away, studying the tiny fragments of broken glass in the sand, breathing the hot scent of the sea, feeling the towel against his cheek, and trying to will away his erection. He should have dug a hole in the sand to make room for it because it felt as if he was lying on a rolling pin.

Shutting his eyes he struggled to think of something boring, his job stocking shelves at the IGA, making sure all the labels faced out, like good little soldiers: canned soup, canned peas, canned tomatoes. Tomatoes. Tomatoes was another word for breasts. But the cans were hard and cold and clammy, just like the IGA where everyone looked deathly pale under the fluorescent lights, especially Norm, the Assistant Manager, a humourless goof who did not appreciate Cyril turning all the labels to the left or to the right, but what else could you do to entertain yourself in such a boring job, a job that Norm seemed to regard as a calling? The pressure in his groin began to ease.

"You're burning."

His eyes opened and he looked up to find Connie leaning over him, smelling sweet and creamy with lotion. "I'm okay," he said.

"Your back's going to get blisters."

"I'm fine."

"Cyril, turn!"

When he did her eyes widened.

"What did you expect?" he said, sullen, defiant, embarrassed.

She drew her finger down the middle of his chest and stopped at his belly button. "Anything less and I'd be insulted." For a long moment they remained that way, looking at each other, her finger circling his navel. He reached up and put his hand on her breast. Her nipple hardened under his touch and she put her hand on his and held it there—then she pushed it away. "I'm sorry, Cyril," she whispered, "but I'm saving myself for my leading man."

THREE

THE NEXT DAY was the start of Grade 12 and Connie didn't show, nor was she there the following day or the day after. She missed the entire week. Each afternoon Cyril detoured past her house but saw no sign of her. Friday he went up the steps and knocked but there was no answer. Cupping his hands around his eyes he peered through the stained glass yet saw nothing.

When he got home he went into the basement. It faced south and the windows were large so it had made a good workshop for his dad. Cyril was ten when his father had died, and he had become obsessed with everything his father had used: razor, brush, hacksaws, screwdrivers, level, chisels, a wood drill with its various bits. Studying each item, weighing them in his hands, smelling them, he was convinced they were imbued with something of his father's essence. He put his father's welding mask on and looked at the world through a grey tint. Was it possible that the mask, having spent so much time on his dad's head, held his dad's thoughts? He began drawing all these things, as if by recreating them he recreated him, or so it seemed, so it felt, and over the years he filled sketch pads with drawings of hammers, saws, torches, boots, subject matter to which he continued to return. Now Cyril had an easel in the basement, his sketch pads and boxes of pencils and charcoal sticks, as well as a mirror and some lights.

He scuffed around the basement wondering what was up with Connie. Wasn't he her leading man? The night she'd come over for supper she'd wanted to see where he worked. That had sounded so mature, so committed: "Where do you work?" As if art was his job. She had looked at everything with great care. When she saw the welding mask she'd put it on and went all stiff like Gort, the robot in *The Day the Earth Stood Still*.

He looked at the jam jars suspended from a plank shelf by a screw through each lid. The jars contained nails and screws and washers and hinges and nuts and bolts. The September sun angling in ignited the hardware in each jar like a row of light bulbs. The basement smelled of metal and concrete. His father's welding equipment stood darkly in a corner: canisters, tubes, torches, even his overalls hung on a nail, all of it as it had been, untouched, as though to interfere with it would be a form of desecration, an unholy attempt to erase his memory. Cyril knew his mother still came down and put her face to his overalls. He'd seen her through the window, leaning there, face to the cloth, an image out of the bible. Cyril had done the same. They worshiped secretly in the cavern of the basement like members of a persecuted sect.

His father had died in 1955. It was not a dramatic death but quiet, like the man himself: he went to bed one night and did not wake up, slipping through a secret door. Cyril's last glimpse of him was in the casket in church, crucifix in his folded hands, carrying an iron flower to the Lord. One of his earliest memories was watching him cut steel with a welding torch. Cyril wasn't supposed to be watching because his father had warned it would damage his eyes, but unable to resist he'd opened the door that led down from the kitchen and peered between the steps, and for the next two days beautiful yellow spots hovered in his vision as though sunflowers were blooming in his eyes. For years afterwards, whenever he visited his dad's grave he'd stare into the sun to relive that.

"At least he outlived that bastard," his mother would always say.

Cyril didn't have to ask who that bastard was. Uncle Joe. Koba the Dread. Any time his mother saw a picture of Stalin in a newspaper, book or magazine, she burned the eyes out with a match. It didn't matter where she was, the waiting room at the doctor's office, the library, a store, out came the matches. More than one person had shouted in alarm and yet she carried right on. Cyril remembered the day he came home from school, up the back steps and into the kitchen and was met by the smell of burning newspaper. There were his dad, his mother, and Paul hunched over a paper speaking low and intense, as if plotting. When they saw Cyril they went quiet. He'd come stumping up the steps but had nonetheless surprised them. Their expressions—round, flat, uncomprehending—said he was a stranger. It was as if he'd stumbled upon their campfire in the forest. Occasionally his dad would start speaking to Cyril in Ukrainian and then catch himself and halt as if he'd let a secret slip, and quickly shift to English. Yet over the years Cyril had heard enough to pick up some of the language, and the afternoon he discovered them hunched over the newspaper he heard Paul say, "Toy proklaty zdoh."

"Who's dead?" asked Cyril.

"No one," said Paul. "Get lost."

"Stalin," said his dad.

Cyril's mother and Paul embraced and sobbed and remained locked together swaying side to side while Cyril's father watched with an expression as unreadable as his welding mask. He needed a shave and his hair was messed and he was in his working greens, and yet here he was, home an hour early. He went to the window. He was about five-foot-eight and broad across the shoulders. Cyril had inherited his sharp chin and large dark eyes. Exhaling hard as if at the end of an ordeal, his dad put his hands on his hips and gazed out, not at the cemetery but at the sky. It was March, almost spring, the sun bright and daffodils blooming. "See." He pointed to a flock of starlings swooping from one maple to another. "The birds are free again."

∽ ∾

It was two weeks before he saw Connie. She showed up at the IGA on a Friday evening carrying an open package of red liquorice whips. She held the package out and he took one. Then she slid the crinkly package up under her black T-shirt and tucked it in. "You won't rat me out will you?"

"Norm'll nail you before you hit the door," said Cyril. He tugged up the hem of her shirt and adjusted it to hide her loot, and as he did he glimpsed her pale smooth stomach, felt its heat against his hands, and wanted to embrace her, but she stepped back out of range.

"Aiding and abetting," she warned.

He'd happily lose his job to win her again.

"So hey," she said, "what happened? You kinda just vanished."

"*Me?*"

Ignoring his shock she twirled her liquorice whip like a lasso. "You drawing?"

Drawing? What was she talking about? "Yeah, some. Sure."

"You're an artist, man. You should draw."

"I'm not an artist," he said, grimly. "I'm just some guy who draws."

She frowned. It was as if an unresolved question had been answered, and Cyril immediately regretted his maudlin statement. She folded liquorice into her mouth then chewed and swallowed and said, "Then that's all you'll ever be." She stated this as if it was a simple if sorrowful fact. For a full minute neither spoke. The muzak drifted down like nerve gas and the fluorescent lights hissed. "Anyhow," she said with exaggerated offhandedness, "I've come to say goodbye." She painted a horizon with a slow pass of her palm, "The distant land of Holy Wood calls to me, *kemosabe*. I must cross many mountains and fight many battles." Then her shoulders sagged and her eyes grew moist and she reached and stroked his cheek. "Besides," she whispered, voice thickening, "if I stay here I'll never get away, I'll never make it." She quickly walked off up the aisle. Before going out the cold glass door with its poster advertising two-for-one frying chickens she turned and aimed her finger at him like a six-shooter. "Draw." Then was gone.

Cyril stood there until Norm tapped him on the back. "Yoo hoo. Chef Boyardee ain't gonna stack himself."

His shift ended an hour later and he went straight to Connie's. The evening was still warm, traffic had lulled and downtown throbbed with a tarnished glow. He walked back and forth in front of her house then went in the gate and up the steps and knocked. The sisal mat said WELCOME. The door opened and a small dark figure appeared on the other side of the screen door. Her grandmother pushed it open and looked him up and down.

"Elle pas d'ici."

"Where is she?" He strained for the French. "Ou est-elle?"

"*Haw*-lee-wood...da da da da da *Haw*-lee-wood."

Cyril ran all the way down the hill, through the cemetery, past Broadway, across the Cambie Bridge and along to the bus station opposite the armoury. Darting amid the buses he read the destinations: Calgary, Prince George, Seattle. He stepped up into the Seattle bus but she wasn't there. He checked the waiting room. Families with suitcases, solitary men with duffel bags, a cat creeping along the wall by the washroom. He dropped to a bench and shut his eyes and counted to ten, thinking that when he opened them she'd be standing there. She wasn't. He did another round of the station. Train. She was going by train. He jogged across the viaduct, in and out of the light of the widely spaced lamp posts, and along Main to the railway station and searched the waiting room and the platforms and even the park across the street and then the station again. No sign of her. He stood with his hands on his hips. He waited there, unmoving, for ten, fifteen, twenty more minutes. If not bus or train then how? Air? It took him an hour to get out to the airport. A flight had left for San Francisco forty minutes earlier—could she have been on it? Or was she hitch-hiking? He imagined her out on the highway, charming a stranger all the way down the coast.

∽ ∾

His mother regarded him with eyes as solemn as gravestones. "You will survive."

He didn't want to survive, there was no point to surviving, surviving was not living it was subsisting, a half-life not worth the effort. He shrugged and said nothing. What was his pain compared to what she'd endured in the war? Anyway, he wasn't merely heartbroken he was bewildered and embarrassed and even a little ashamed because clearly he wasn't enough for Connie, or—and this was a shock—maybe he was too much, and would smother her career before it even had a chance to grow.

And another thing tormented him. When she'd left the store he should have gone after her right away, not waited another hour for his shift to end. Why had he hesitated? What did that say about him? Maybe she'd been out there waiting—hoping— to see if he'd come after her, to see if he really loved her?

Cyril found himself contemplating suicide. Hanging was too grimly messy, drowning was too wet and cold, pills and booze he'd probably convulse and vomit, he couldn't bring himself to jump head first out of a tree—certainly not their tree—which left shooting himself, which meant finding a gun.

As a boy he'd often imagined shooting Hitler and Stalin, sniper style, from the window of a bombed-out building. He'd wait patiently in the rain or snow or dust, through days and nights, though never would his resolve weaken, and then the moment would come when the Fuhrer or Koba raced past to a meeting of generals. He'd take aim. Tick. The rifle bullet pierces the Führer's skull right behind the ear and the Führer's head flops forward. Tick. Uncle Joe topples against the shoulder of his aide. Later, in London, Churchill would decorate him, and his mother and father would be there watching, and even Paul would have to give Cyril his due.

Not that his mother and father wanted reminders of the war. They'd avoided the prairies where so many Eastern Europeans congregated and come all the way out to Vancouver to escape getting caught up in an enclave that might have kept those wounds open. Paul had told him that, one of the few bits of info about the family prehistory that he'd shared. Another was the fact that the word slave came from Slav. "Vikings navigated the rivers from the Baltic into Russia," he said. "All the way to Kiev, kidnapping locals on the way and selling them to Turks who'd come up from the Black Sea."

Ukrainians tended to be tall and fair-skinned; Paul looked like an emaciated Peter Lorre, and while Cyril was bigger and healthier he was no tall blond. "What happened to us?"

"What happened to us? I'll tell you what happened to us. While the Turkish slave buyers were waiting around in Kiev they got horny so went to the whorehouses, and guess what happened? Us!"

He could never tell when Paul was lying or being brutally honest. For as long as Cyril could remember his older brother had banked on Cyril's naïveté: heads I win, tails you lose, chocolate milk came from brown cows, cats were female dogs, the moon was the sun with its back turned, they used to put bells in coffins so that if you got buried alive you could ring for help, Hitler was a vegetarian. Some of it turned out to be true and some BS. The Lone Ranger and Tonto were homosexuals. That one had thrown him for a loop and he'd never watched the show the same way again.

On television there were WASPs and Italians and Irish, as if the whole world was comprised of those three groups. Movies were a little more diverse with some token Jews, Negroes and Chinese sprinkled around the edges, though scarcely any Eastern Europeans at all, and if there were they were Commie spies or coal miners: sweaty, grimy and grim, like Stanley Kowalski, the lummox in *A Streetcar Named Desire*.

Subhumans. *Untermenschen*. The Nazi term for Slav, beasts destined to serve.

The first time Gilbert heard Cyril's parents speak Ukrainian he was appalled. "What're they doing?" he'd complained, the disgust in his voice tangible, his nose wrinkling as though the very language itself did not merely sound strange but smelled strange. Gilbert McNab's view was that the world spoke English, only Krauts and Commies grunted like animals. And there was more than merely the language, there was the cabbage and garlic. Gilbert grimaced and waved his hand in front of his face. "Farts."

FOUR

SIX MONTHS AFTER Connie vanished Cyril finally got hold of a gun thanks to Gilbert's grandmother. Cyril had known the old lady for as long as he could remember, a tiny, trembly woman with an enormous head covered in wispy hair that looked like the dust that collected under beds. She spent her time in the middle of the living room couch sucking butterscotch sweeties in front of the TV; her Glaswegian brogue was all but incomprehensible, as if she was talking with a sock in her throat. When she died a jewellery box went into the coffin with her. Gilbert became obsessed with it, imagining money, gold, diamonds.

For weeks after she was buried Gilbert brought flowers each day to her grave. Sometimes Gilbert popped over in the morning on the way to school; other times he went over late at night. Her grave was right next to her husband's, Gilbert's grandfather, who'd blown his own brains out.

Cyril's mother, who had no great opinion of Gilbert, remarked with wonder upon his devotion. "There he is again," she said, peering out the kitchen window at Gilbert's silhouette. "He loved her." There was bewilderment in her voice. Cyril too was surprised. Gilbert had always referred to the old lady as *what's her nuts*. As in, *what's her nuts* was crabbin' at me again. Or, *what's her nuts* was in the can all night. Or, *what's her nuts* hit me with her fuckin' cane.

It was March, 1963, and as the days got longer Gilbert's visits got later and later so that he was often there at midnight or beyond. Cyril was careful not to pry.

While Gilbert attended his grandmother's grave, Cyril lay awake wondering what Connie was doing at that very moment in Los Angeles: working late at some waitressing job, rehearsing lines for a part, or—and this caused his gut to knot—was she with a lover, her leading man . . . He imagined going down there and finding her. He could support himself by sitting in parks and drawing portraits. He'd seen guys doing that here in Stanley Park on Sundays. Not a glorious artistic career, but down there in LA, in Hollywood, he could get discovered. He envisioned Elvis Presley or Steve McQueen strolling by with a starlet on their arm pausing to admire Cyril's stuff and maybe even getting their own portrait done: word would get around and just like that Cyril would be made. It happened all the time in Hollywood, didn't it? He thought of Natalie Wood's character in *Gypsy*. Whenever he watched TV he paid particular attention to crowd scenes and peripheral characters, thinking he might spot Connie, but there weren't many Orientals on television, just Fuji on *McHale's Navy* and some extras on *The Hawaiian Eye*.

One night Cyril saw Gilbert pushing through the hedge into the cemetery packing something long over his shoulder. Cyril got dressed and went on over to join him. A chill drizzle fell and downtown glowed cold and grey. As he approached he heard dull thumps and muted cursing, so circled cautiously around the grave and saw a head on the ground—Gilbert's head. All manner of explanation raced through Cyril's mind, the chief of which was that Gilbert had been decapitated, though the reality was that he was standing in a hole.

Gilbert greeted Cyril cheerfully. "Hey, buddy."

"Hey."

"Dump this, will you?" Gilbert hoisted two pails of dirt up and out of the hole onto the grass.

Cyril lugged the pails to the hedge and emptied them. When he got back he heard the thump of a shovel blade striking wood.

"Drill."

Cyril found a manual wood drill in a gunny sack. A dull grinding followed.

"Saw."

Cyril passed down the saw and soon came the rasp of steel teeth on hard wood.

"Mask."

Cyril found a gauze mask smelling of vanilla extract. The furious sawing resumed. Half an hour ago he'd been in bed and now it seemed he was robbing a grave. Cyril knew he should go home, just slip away quietly, but the lure of Gilbert had always been the lure of the unexpected, the mildly larcenous or outright criminal, and it overrode any qualms regarding sacrilege or fear of punishment, divine or otherwise.

Gilbert crawled out of the hole with a small wooden box. He saw Cyril's horrified expression.

"It's not robbery. She was my grandmother. It's family property." They covered the hole with boards and sod. Tools clanking, they retreated to Cyril's basement where Gilbert gave the enigmatic wooden box a shake: whatever was inside was padded. Now Gilbert took needle-nose pliers from the sack and with one twist cranked off the lock, splintering the wood in the process. He lifted the lid revealing a velvet cloth of royal blue with gold trim then, like a groom about to raise his bride's veil, he lifted the edge of the cloth: a pistol. Old, perhaps army issue, it had a grooved Vulcanite hand grip. Gilbert opened the cylinder and discovered four bullets. He and Cyril looked at each other in exhilarated terror. An empty gun was hardware; a loaded gun was a weapon. Each turn of the cylinder caused a rich steely click. Gilbert weighed the gun's lethal heft and his eyes gleamed at the range of dark possibilities now open before him. Yet one realization dominated the rest. He looked at Cyril and in a voice of quiet wonder said, "This is the gun my grandfather killed himself with. It has to be. Why else would what's her nuts have kept it?"

Cyril had no idea why else. But a different thought hit him. "Hey, now you can kill yourself."

"Yeah," Gilbert drawled. "Could do."

"Temple or mouth?"

Gilbert blew air. "Probably doesn't make all that much diff. Temple I guess. Don't much like the idea of sucking on a pistol barrel. Might do it in the cemetery on a full moon." Then he grew philosophical as he gazed at the gun. "Of course, I would like to lose my virginity first. Maybe I'll meet her when I'm standing there with the gun to my temple," said Gilbert—*her* being the girl who finally took pity on him and gave him sex— "And her heart goes out to me because she recognizes the depth of my soul and sees that I'm noble, that I've got potential, that I'm a fucking genius, and she talks me out of it. And she's like the daughter of some shipping magnate who hates me at first and threatens to disown her, but I show him what I'm made of, that we're similar him and me, and I'll be his protégé, and he'll take me on and I'll inherit everything."

It was an impressively impassioned monologue. Maybe Gilbert should have tried acting, though he might have connected with Connie. The only thing worse than losing Connie would have been losing her to Gilbert. Cyril thought of Gilbert calling Connie up and trying to steal her away from him. Cyril had never said anything, though he didn't forget. "Then you won't need the gun and you can lend it to me."

Knowing how heartbroken Cyril had been, he said, "Maybe if you only maim yourself and Connie hears about it she'll come back."

"Actually, I was thinking of shooting Darrel."

ᖋ ᖌ

Darrel was Cyril's mother's boyfriend. They'd met at a Christmas party at the Ukrainian Hall and for reasons Cyril was having difficulty understanding his mother had been seeing him for three months. On Fridays Darrel took her to the Legion and on Sundays he came to dinner, with the result that Cyril had come to dread Sundays. That she should be having sex constituted the deepest imaginable betrayal of his father, even if he had been dead ten years. Cyril understood that she was lonely, but he did not understand that she should do anything about it, certainly not with a guy like Darrel.

"Hey, bub."

"Hey."

Darrel was stretched out full-length on their couch, one of his mother's embroidered pillows under his head, shoes off exposing his red and blue diamond-check socks, ankles crossed. He was vice principal and Guidance Counsellor at some high school. Short and portly, with male pattern baldness, Darrel favoured western wear: string ties, cowboy boots, and shirts embroidered with lariat motifs. No one resembled a cowboy less than Darrel, yet not only had he grown up on a ranch, he was a war hero, having won a Distinguished Service Medal, and for two years he'd been a kicker for the Edmonton Eskimos. The first time they met, Darrel had demonstrated his kicking prowess by setting up Cyril's football in a convenient knothole on the back porch then sailing it out across the alley and into the cemetery. It was January, and he'd made the kick in his socks. He'd stepped back three paces, given his arms a shake, then darted forward with the precision of the expert and kicked. Darrel already had a Players out of his pack and fired up when the ball binged off a gravestone fifty yards away then rolled another thirty down the slope. "Not half-bad for a fat old fart, eh?" Cyril was stuck with the chore of retrieving the ball. When he got back he found Darrel and his mother necking. His mother—*necking*. In English class they were reading *Heart of Darkness*, and two words came to mind: *the horror*. Cyril stashed the ball in the basement, determined that Darrel would never touch it again. If only he could dispose of Darrel as simply.

Darrel said, "Got you some info here." With his chin he indicated a stack of catalogues on the coffee table.

Cyril picked one up. The University of Toronto. There was also one for Dalhousie, for the University of British Columbia, and for Simon Fraser University, a new school right here in the Lower Mainland due to open in the fall. Cyril had no intention of going to any of these places. "Great. Thanks."

"You're most very welcome indeed young sir."

Cyril's mother had squeezed herself onto the end of the couch and positioned Darrel's feet on her thighs. The gallant Darrel gave her the cigarette from his mouth and lit another for himself. She'd never smoked before; now she puffed away like a pro, wrist cocked in a burlesque of elegance.

Darrel was indicating the catalogues again. "How about pharmacy? I'd go in for pharmacy if I was your age. No sticking your fingers in unsavoury places like doctors and veterinarians, if you get my meaning. But you'll need to work on your math and your chemistry," he warned. "I hear you're not exactly an academic. Not that that's an insurmountable hurdle. Wasn't for me, and I was a lousy student. Ds and Cs all the way. Most everyone had me pegged for a broom jockey. But when I finally got a direction—" He nodded slowly as if to say look out, a bull was on the charge. "I worked hard. Direction. That's the key."

Cyril tried to look enthralled by this gripping saga.

"All you need is drive; drive and direction. They go together. I know it's tough. Seems uphill all the way. But you don't want to end up in Fraser Mills the rest of your life. You don't want to end up on the green chain."

The green chain was the quicksand of jobs—put your toe in and it sucked you down and you never escaped. And it was easy to fall in because of that union wage: one, two, three, you had a car and a wife and a mortgage and it was bye-bye dreams, see you in forty years when you retired, unless, that is, the job killed you first, or took off your arm, and left you like a war vet in the legion watching the bubbles in your beer, boring everyone with your tale of woe.

"I can recommend a tutor," said Darrel. "Ooh..."

Cyril's mother had begun massaging Darrel's feet and was now cracking his toes, working her way from the smallest to the biggest. She'd never rubbed his dad's feet.

"Yeah," admitted Darrel. "You're at a tough age. Big changes. Big decisions. In the Norse sagas a man's soul is but a bird in a storm." He sighed smoke and watched it drift.

Their existential reflection was broken by the sound of footsteps on the back porch. Paul appeared with Della, the woman Cyril had first seen in the café last summer. They were now engaged. Della had just finished nursing school and was already working at VGH. She'd been a swimmer and had broad shoulders and narrow hips and tonight she was wearing toreador pants and a matching jacket. She and her mother-in-law promptly disappeared into the kitchen.

"We're sorting out number two son's future here," Darrel informed Paul. Darrel was upright now and had discovered that his rye on the rocks was empty. He jingled the ice in the glass as if ringing a bell. "Pardon me, miss. Any chance of a refill?"

Cyril and Paul watched their mother hurry in and take the glass and return a minute later with a fresh one.

"So what do you think, Paul? Pharmacy?"

Cyril braced himself for a two-on-one attack.

"I don't know if that's quite where Cyril's strengths lie," Paul said, suddenly judicious.

"Is that right?" Darrel was disappointed at not finding an instant ally, but intrigued as well.

Cyril was interested—and fearful—of learning where, in Paul's opinion, his strengths lay. He could hear the laughter if he told them he was intending to go to art school. Both Darrel and Paul were looking at him. To his own surprise he stated: "Maybe I'll join the navy."

"*The navy?*" Cyril's mother had been listening from the kitchen.

"Why not?" he asked, suddenly liking the sound of it. Maybe it would involve travel to tropical ports. Hadn't Gauguin gone to Tahiti? If Connie could run off why not him?

"Well, you get seasick for one thing," his mother said.

Paul was laughing. "He threw up on the ferry to Victoria."

Cyril was scalded. They'd boarded the boat in the downtown harbour and halfway across the strait he was vomiting.

Darrel liked what he was hearing. The troops were back in order. "Maybe the army, eh bub. Keep your feet on the ground."

"Ginger's good for motion sickness," offered Della.

They were on dessert when his mother asked if he'd heard from Connie, as if she was only off on a bit of a jaunt. He considered lying then just shook his head.

"No big movie contracts?" enquired Darrel.

His mother had blabbed. He felt invaded and betrayed, and for the rest of the meal stayed silent.

"She's waiting for the right role," said Paul. "The Queen of Kowloon."

"Sounds like a ship," said Darrel.

"Yeah, a laundry boat."

"Maybe her ship will come in," said the ever optimistic Della. They all looked at her, not sure if she was witty or naive. Cyril wondered why she'd married Paul.

Later that evening, when Darrel was gone, Paul directed Cyril downstairs into the basement for a few words. They leaned against the old workbench, arms crossed, under the bare bulb.

"I've been doing a little research on Mr Darrel Stavrik," said Paul. "Looked through the Edmonton directory then made a few calls." His smile would have terrified Cyril in any other circumstances, but now he leaned forward eager to hear what he'd dug up. "Bugger has a wife and five kids."

"Five?"

"Five."

Being married was bad enough, having a kid was bad enough, but five of them? "The bastard."

"I'd love to see him get audited," said Paul, who looked almost dreamy at the thought of Darrel sweating before an Inquisition of Accountants. Cyril could see Paul seated at a high bench in black robes and a ruffled collar glowering ominously as he aimed an accusing finer. "Could be time to dial a few numbers."

At that moment Cyril admired his older brother. Rare were the times they were on the same side but this was one and he was proud.

"Still, mom likes him," admitted Paul, sobering.

"She's changing," said Cyril. "It's like she's not even her anymore."

"Maybe she's glad not to be her anymore," said Della, coming down the steps. She had a long face and long teeth, a thin nose between big eyes, and straight brown hair through which her ears poked, though for all this she was not unattractive. She looked to Cyril like some sort of doll fashioned from sticks and straw.

"Do you like him?" he asked her.

She shrugged. "Your mother does and that's what counts."

Cyril genuinely liked Della, yet her relentless reasonableness was too much. "He's pushy."

Della leaned to look at Cyril's sketch of Connie. She was gazing forthrightly out from the paper as if committing Cyril to memory, as if Connie was doing the portrait, not Cyril. "Forget the Navy," said Della. "Go to art school." Before this became a general topic of discussion—and inevitably ridicule—she turned to Paul and reminded him she had the early shift tomorrow.

When Paul and Della were gone Cyril's mother asked him to sit down.

He knew what was coming.

"Darrel's only trying to help."

"I don't want his help."

"You'll be moving out some day and I'll be on my own. I'm thinking of the future. *My* future."

His heart clenched and for the first time he saw her as she saw herself: a forty-four-year-old widow about to be abandoned. Widow. What a desolate word. Yet he could not accept Darrel living here in the house Cyril had lived all his life, where his memories resided. Darrel, King of the Manor. No. It was wrong.

The following Sunday, Cyril waited for Paul to drop the bomb and announce the news of Darrel's other family. They went through the roast beef and the apple pie then the coffee and he still hadn't raised the subject. Cyril caught Paul's eye and saw that he was playing innocent. Cyril suspected that Della had put a gag order on him. Cyril dove in, "So, Darrel, how's the family? In Edmonton."

"They're doing just fine," he said. "Thank you for asking."

"Your wife?" repeated Cyril.

"Fine as far as I know."

Their mother was smiling, perfectly at ease dating a married man with five children.

∾　∾

"You don't have to like him," she said later.

"He's always calling me bub."

"Is just his way."

"I don't like his way."

"He's willing to put you through university."

"Who said I'm going to university?"

"Then trade school."

"Why him?"

"I should sit home alone?"

"He's married."

"She left him."

"He's got kids."

"So do I."

Why could he never win an argument with her? It was as if he was forever five years old. The row of Virgin Marys on the mantel seemed to be smirking. He risked the question he feared the most: "Are you going to marry him?"

He saw lament and anger and exhaustion on her face; worst of all he saw that he was boring her.

☞ ☜

All that week Cyril practised aiming Gilbert's pistol, one eye closed, right hand supported by his left, breath smooth and slow and even. "Firm the shoulder and exhale when you squeeze the trigger." His dad had taught him these basics using Cyril's six-shooter cap gun. He and his dad had often played guns in the basement, ducking in and around the furnace and the stacked boxes. His dad never lasted long in the game, saying that the snap-snap-snap of the caps gave him a headache, and it was only years later that Cyril realized it was more than the mere noise that caused him to shut his eyes and rub his temples and withdraw to the bedroom and shut the door.

Darrel was surprised but genial the Saturday Cyril showed up at his apartment. He got him a stubby of Black Label, half of which Cyril drank in one chug, Darrel nodding as if impressed by such drinking bravado. The place smelled of coffee and cigarettes. On the wall above the couch hung a landscape of horses running away over hills.

"So what's up, bub?"

Cyril belched and said, "Leave my mother alone," then belched again.

Darrel relaxed on the couch and lit up a smoke. "Sit down."

Cyril shook his head.

Darrel puffed reflectively. "You really hate me, huh?"

The quiet wonder in Darrel's voice made Cyril reflect. Paul

hated him, or often resented his youth and health with a hate-like intensity, and now he couldn't help feeling a little bad at hurting Darrel's feelings. "I just want you to leave her alone."

"I don't think she wants me to leave her alone. Have you considered that?"

Cyril gulped the rest of the beer and reached down and carefully set the bottle on the coffee table. As a matter of fact he had considered that—he just refused to accept it.

"You want another one of those?"

"No." He'd gulped too fast and some of the beer was rising back up his nose. He fought not to cough.

"Your mother wants to forget it all. The old country, the war, the past, the whole shootin' match." Darrel gestured dismissively. "Time to move on. And definitely time to move out of that house with the front row seat of the graveyard."

So that was it. Erase his past, erase his father and take his mother and sell the house. Cyril pulled out the gun.

Darrel began to chuckle. He stretched out his short legs and crossed his ankles and got comfortable. Darrel was always getting comfy. "We could get along, you know. Ever consider that?"

He and Darrel, pals? Maybe catch a Lions game? Darrel might have connections and Cyril could meet the players, shake hands with Joe Kapp and Willie Fleming. Yet this too he couldn't accept. Cyril aimed the pistol.

"You're starting to bug me, kid." Darrel flicked his cigarette hitting Cyril in the chest. He flinched but kept the pistol pointed and could see the butt smouldering on the hardwood. Unable to restrain himself he crushed it out with his toe.

Darrel sighed. He stood and tugged up his trousers. He was big-bellied but broad-shouldered and had burly forearms, an old, short, bald athlete. "Now you can hit the road and we'll say no more about this or I can kick your can around the block."

Cyril fought the impulse to obey, knowing that if he backed down now Darrel would be top dog forever. He kept the pistol steady.

"I'm getting bored, bub."

"Don't call me bub."

"You're bub until you start acting like an adult. Now swing your arse around and hop it on out the door before I tell mommy what you've been up to with your cap gun."

Cyril exhaled and squeezed the trigger slowly. The bullet blasted the floor between Darrel's stocking feet. Darrel went straight up, squeaking like a shot rat. A small giggle escaped Cyril's mouth, then another burp.

"You dumb little fuck!" Darrel shrank back behind his Danish modern couch.

"Bang," said Cyril, "you're dead." And blew imaginary smoke from the barrel.

∽ ∾

Days passed while Cyril waited for the cops to show. They didn't. His mother didn't see Darrel that Friday, nor did Darrel show on Sunday. She didn't say anything about it. Was she secretly relieved? Did she realize it was for the best? Cyril hadn't told anyone what he'd done; he could scarcely believe it himself. When he'd returned the pistol Gilbert had noted the missing bullet and Cyril said he'd fired at a crow in the cemetery.

Another week passed. If Darrel had said anything to Cyril's mother she was doing a good job of keeping it to herself. He watched for clues but she was unreadable; apparently she had interior rooms opening onto ever deeper rooms, where memories resided like refugees in a labyrinth. When Paul and Della took Cyril aside and asked what had become of Darrel he tried not looking shifty and said who knew, ask mom, and when Paul did just that she looked out the window at the cemetery and after a moment of silence, during which Cyril tensed in fear, she said, "He's gone, like everyone else."

ဗ္ဓာ   ဓာ

Growing cocky with relief, Cyril resumed turning the tins of Chef Boyardee at the IGA so that entire rows looked to the right, or half the row looked to the right and half to the left, or he alternated stacking them upside down and right side up, prompting Norm to ask if he was a retard. Cyril crossed his eyes and said yes. Norm got Barnes, the manager, who regarded Cyril's handiwork and after a moment's cogitation asked if Cyril liked his job.

"Not really." Dizzy at his own brazenness, he asked Barnes, "Do you like your job?"

Barnes had a crewcut, a belly that strained his white shirt, a five o'clock shadow that looked like iron filings, and yet was not unintelligent or utterly without a measure of charm. Cyril had often seen him joshing with customers, especially the ladies, who seemed to find him curiously engaging despite his pallor. Barnes barked a laugh and shook his head and said, "No one likes their job, kid. Except maybe Hughie Hefner. Stack 'em straight or quit."

Barnes was perfectly at ease with his station in life, an ease which Cyril envied. That was the thing about adults, or most of them; even the dumbest seemed to have dealt with the issues of women and money and career. Produce Manager Norm spent his day spritzing lettuce and celery and yet he also had a wife and a kid and a house and—even Cyril had to admit—a sort of a life.

FIVE

CYRIL GRADUATED WITH a 2.5 Grade Point Average, his A+ in Art and his A in Phys. Ed. compensating for the C minuses in Math and Chemistry. His mother urged him to go for a plumbing apprenticeship but he didn't like the idea of putting his arm down toilets or up pipes. She suggested electrician but the very thought of watts and volts and amps agitated his nerves. As for welding it was haunted. Carpentry, she said, and he shrugged meaning maybe, and then devoted the summer to a series of drawings for his art school application: eight postage stamps, two feet by three, of Stalin. In one Stalin was dancing like a dervish, arms out, head tilted, eyes shut, the cancellation mark functioning like lines of motion accentuating the sense of spinning, a detail about which he was rather proud even though it had been a lucky accident. In another he was sitting with his legs straight out, wearing a diaper, a gigantic infant biting the head off a man clenched like a lollipop in his fist. Some of the pictures were pencil and some were coloured chalk. He liked the dry quality of chalk because Stalin was a creature of sand and grit and dust, his soul smoke. The last drawing, as yet unfinished, was still on the easel. It showed a laughing Stalin on a swing, wearing baby shoes, kicking out his pudgy bare legs, bonnet on his head. It echoed a memory of being on a swing with his father pushing, one of the few times Cyril recalled his dad laughing loudly and without restraint.

That summer he went to see *Moulin Rouge* starring Jose Ferrer as Toulouse Lautrec, fascinated by the crippled artist and his suicidal capacity for absinthe. He saw *The Moon and Six-pence* on TV and admired the expat painter Charles Strickland's brazen drunk indifference to everything, including the man who wanted to buy his work. What confidence, what clarity, what perverse defiance. Then there was a film on Van Gogh in which he eats a tube of paint. Cyril had no desire to eat paint, but he envied those three men their focus and energy, their drive and direction; they knew who they were and where they were going and nothing was getting in their way. They did not merely accept their calling, they pursued it, ran it down like wolves. He found an autobiography by Salvador Dali, a man who was as eccentric as surrealism itself. In it Dali pours honey down his chest so he can study the flies that come to feed. One morning after his mother left for work and Cyril had a few hours before his shift at the IGA, he got the honey from the cupboard ready to do his own Salvador Dali. Unfortunately, it was creamed honey, solid. He carved some from the jar with a knife and smoothed it over his chest and lay back in bed with the window open. He heard lawn mowers and the opening and closing of hearse doors in the cemetery. Finally one fly came bumbling in and landed on him and got stuck, one wing whirring pathetically. Eventually another fly circled and got stuck, then a bee, then two more flies. Cyril watched them buzz and struggle. Now what? Was this Existential? He took a shower, still not quite sure what the crazy Spaniard was on about, and wondering if this lack of understanding was a lack of artistic vision.

With just a week to go before the art school entrance interview, Cyril came home from his shift at the IGA one evening and discovered all eight drawings missing. He found his mother watching TV.

"...My drawings..."

"They're gone," she said.

"I kind of noticed that. Where have they gone *to*?"

She shrugged and kept her eyes on Charlie McCarthy and Edgar Bergen. Cyril watched her watch, then abruptly started searching. The fireplace was clean. The pail under the sink was empty. He went out and looked in the garbage can: nothing.

"Draw flowers or fruit," she said when he came back in. "People like flowers and fruit. They put them on their walls. Do some nice sunflowers and I'll buy them."

Cyril searched the closets, the attic, behind the furnace. From downstairs he shouted up through the main floor. "I worked hard on those, ma!" He pounded back up the steps and into the living room.

On the TV screen the wooden dummy's jaw clacked mockingly up and down. "Why do you have to keep him alive?" she asked.

"I'm going to miss the application deadline."

"You know what he did."

"Are pictures that powerful?"

"He starved us."

Cyril was stymied. "I worked hard on them..." He heard how hollow his words sounded.

"Three million."

"They were mine."

She was wearing a black cardigan and smoking a cigarette—a habit she'd maintained after Darrel left—feet in their hen-feather slippers on the grey Formica coffee table next to the *Province* and a stack of *Reader's Digest*s. She turned back to the TV. "Better you get trade."

"You hate me."

"You are my son."

"You still hate me."

She turned her head slowly like a tank turret and aimed her gaze at him, her eyes wet but tearless, her voice steady. "I love you."

"It's revenge. You're getting back at me."

She swivelled her gaze back to the TV.

"I'll draw them again."

"Draw, don't draw. Just don't let me see."

∽   ∾

The interviewer frowned at the picture Cyril had drawn that very morning, torn from his sketchbook and mounted on poster board. The man took up another of the same subject, a be-robed owl whirling dervish-wise, wings out, head tipped, eyes closed. There was a copy of the giddy Stalin on a child's swing, wearing a bonnet, a soother in his mouth. He'd intended to redo his entire Stalin series but was afraid his mother would destroy them again. He'd got onto owls for no other reason than that Gilbert had bought a stuffed one from the St. Vincent de Paul as a joke and named it Elvis.

"You handle a pencil reasonably well," admitted the interviewer, a pale man with lank brown hair, a posh British accent, and nicotine-stained fingernails. "They've got verve. But they're hasty. They're rushed."

Cyril started to explain what had happened but the other interviewer, a fat man in a black turtleneck, black beard, and black crewcut, seemed in no mood for explanations. He pooched out his wet, red lips then sucked them back in. "Impatience is the mark of the amateur." *Ama-toor.*

"Not uninteresting though," allowed the first. "Intriguing, actually."

"Makes me want to scrub my hands with bleach," said the fat one. "And there's no colour. Nowhere do I see colour." He sorted through the drawings with his thick-fingered hands. "Drawing and colour are not distinct. As one paints, one draws. Can you tell me who said that?"

Cyril could not.

"Cezanne. When colour is richest, form is most complete."

"Many fine artists have worked in a limited palette," said the first.

The other was unimpressed. "Adolescent," he said, pointing to Stalin in the bonnet. He turned his profile to Cyril, indicating that the interview was at an end.

"That's a tad harsh, Glen."

Glen gazed at the door as though longing to obey the EXIT sign above it. "Alistair, dishonesty serves no one."

Alistair clasped his hands on the desk and looked seriously at Cyril. "Why do you draw?"

"It's as if there's always something waiting at the end of the drawing," he said. "Something surprising."

Alistair nodded vigorously.

"The question," said Glen, turning his gaze from the EXIT sign back to Cyril, "is whether you've got any vision worth evolving. Otherwise you are merely a draughtsman."

"Draughtsmanship is important," cautioned Alistair.

"But without vision it is merely a trade," said Glen.

"My father was a draughtsman," said Alistair. He nodded encouragingly to Cyril. "There's a call for draughtsman in the building industry. Have you considered draughting?"

≈   ≈

That September he moved into the top floor of an old house with slanted ceilings and a view of rooftops and downtown, the closest thing to a Parisian garret the city had to offer. He continued stocking shelves at the IGA and with the rest of his time he drew, occasionally venturing into colour, doing oil pastels of the city at night while listening to the traffic, the sirens, the shouts, the occasional crump of a collision or crack of a gunshot.

He imagined Connie living here with him. She could hang her swords on the wall, he'd help her rehearse her lines, and she'd pose for him. He phoned her house once but her grandmother just kept repeating, "*Je ne connais pas. C'est vie pas bon, pas bon . . .*"

Then Paul showed up one evening. This would have been

awkward at the best of times, but the fact that he was drunk made it worse. Paul was erratic when he drank and tended to say even more vicious things than when sober, but this time booze had put him in a maudlin mood; he looked old and tired and troubled; he'd never had many friends and it was terrifying for Cyril to realize that after a lifetime of enduring Paul's sarcasm he was turning to him. It was a first, and Cyril wasn't sure how to act.

Sensing Cyril's unease, Paul reverted to form. "This place is a hole."

Cyril was almost grateful. "Nice to see you, too."

Paul raised his middle finger and kissed it. "Any time. Got anything to drink?"

"Tap water."

Paul sneered then drew a flask from his suit coat, swigged, and was halfway through twisting the cap back on before he paused and tilted it toward Cyril.

"What is it?"

"Chinese tea. What difference does it make?"

Cyril drank. Whisky. He suppressed a grimace and passed it back.

Paul gave it a shake to see how much was left then gulped the remainder. "She's miserable."

At first Cyril thought he meant Della. Then he understood. "Ma?"

He nodded heavily. "Misses him."

"Dad?"

"Darrel," said Paul, shaking his head in disgust.

"What does she say?"

"Doesn't have to say anything. I can see it in her face."

Cyril guiltily changed the subject and asked after Della.

Paul gestured as if to say who knew. "Swimming, volleyball, archery."

Cyril could see Della, tall, strong, focused, shooting a bow and arrow.

"Next it'll be lacrosse."

Paul wore glasses with thick black frames and a short-sleeved button down white shirt and narrow black tie. Mr. CGA. Paul looked up suddenly. "I miss the old man."

"Me too."

"You knew he was a party member?"

"No."

"No?"

Paul's tone angered Cyril. "How could I? No one ever told me anything. You guys all made sure of that."

Paul shrugged and looked out the window. "Okay, okay. I'm not here so you can gripe. That's why they left Lvov and moved east, to Kiev. To be closer to the centre. Closer to him, the great man. Everyone wanted to be near him." Paul yanked at his tie loosening it. "He was a god. The new god. And the old man was a believer. He believed it all. The people, fed and happy and singing." He grew quiet, adding, "Dad loved to sing."

Cyril didn't remember his father ever singing and had a hard time even imagining it. "What about ma?"

Paul blew air and shrugged. "She believed because he believed. Because it was exciting. Because it was big. Because it was history. They figured believe hard enough they could make it real. That if you didn't believe there was something wrong with you. And if you didn't you ended up in a camp or against a wall. So they believed. Except Koba wasn't much of a god. Not even much of an uncle. He stole the harvests. Let the Ukrainians starve, better to feed the people in Moscow, the people who count. The winter of frozen corpses. Ma told me about it. Every morning the streets and the river bank thick with bodies frozen as hard as marble. The rats couldn't even chew them. The ears. They could chew the ears. Went on all through the '30s and then the war. The thing is if they'd have stayed in Lvov we'd have been able to eat. And maybe my bones wouldn't be like balsa wood." He shut his eyes and slumped back, exhausted. "You, you're lucky. Did you know there's a town in Ukraine called Luck?"

Cyril walked past Darrel's place, a two-storey, stucco-sided apartment building with junipers and bark mulch. It was early evening. Cyril walked past twice. On the third pass he plunged on up the walk to the intercom and ran his finger down the list of names and discovered that where Stavrik had been there was now a strip of masking tape with 'Occupant' written in red ink. He stepped back to see the front of the building, thinking he might spot some clue. Nothing. He returned to the intercom, took a breath and pressed the buzzer. It ticked and buzzed, ticked and buzzed. He was relieved until he knew he'd have to return and try again later, so he buzzed again and counted ten ticks. As he was turning to leave, a female voice broke through the static.

Had Darrel already hooked up with another woman? He felt betrayed on his mother's behalf. How long had it been, six months? He leaned towards the grille and asked if Darrel was there.

"Who?" The woman sounded young, his age.

The bastard was playing around with one of his students! "Darrel Stavrik," he repeated.

"Oh, him. I don't know. I heard he moved back to Edmonton. To his wife."

⚮ ⚭

Gilbert often dropped by after driving cab. They'd drink Luckys and stare out the window speculating on their futures, Gilbert in no doubt that his future was bright and full of money, that he was destined to make a million before he was thirty.

"Driving hack?"

Smiling at such simplicity, Gilbert said, "It's research, my friend. Making contact with people who count."

"Like who?"

Gilbert became enigmatic—one of his favourite roles—and said he was meeting big wheels, high-fliers, movers and shakers, entrepreneurs, managers and CEOs, people who were going places, and he was taking notes. "Don't worry about me, my friend, worry about yourself."

⚮ ⚭

Entering the desolation of the IGA one afternoon Cyril heard the muzak—Acker Bilk doing *Stranger on the Shore*. He cringed under the bleached light of the fluorescent tubes, felt the skin-constricting chill of the refrigerated air, sensed the tins of Chef Boyardee watching him, endured the mockery of the Jolly Green Giant, saw Norm spritzing the iceberg lettuce. Cyril stood as if in a coma. He couldn't muster a thought, he could feel though, and what he felt was despair. Was this his Fraser Mills, his green chain? Water splattered his face.

"Start stacking." Norm's crewcut resembled the bristles of a scrub brush and his eyes were pebbles, hard and small and dark.

Cyril started to speak but didn't know what to say so turned and walked out.

He began looking for jobs. He considered Hotel/Motel Management, Small Arms Repair, Power Engineering, careers he'd seen advertised on the inside cover of a matchbook. He investigated the possibility of becoming a dental mechanic, thinking that making false teeth involved an element of sculpting. He pondered and rejected taxidermy, just as he rejected Mortuary Arts, both of which had a certain aesthetic component. He got hired on as an apprentice upholsterer but quit after six days because the formaldehyde in the fabric gave him headaches. He began training to be a bus driver but quit realizing the scores of rude, violent, weirdos he'd have to deal with. He got on at a pallet mill, a shingle mill, a paper mill, a foundry, the brewery, a distillery, an office that did phone sales, a hospital. An earnest pursuit of employment evolved into a game, the highlight of which was finding and quitting two jobs in one day; in the morning getting hired on at an automotive parts warehouse and in the afternoon a rope factory. He worked as a swamper, a garbage man, a night janitor, a mail sorter. He installed windows, laid carpet, assembled lawn chairs, filled out the paperwork for training as a fireman. He enjoyed this whirlwind of possible careers. Quitting jobs was exhilarating. Everyone was hiring. He even sold, for an afternoon, the

Encyclopaedia Britannica door to door. One thing he never did, however, was wash dishes. It was only when Gilbert urged him to try getting into the *Guinness Book of World Records* for the most jobs ever that Cyril decided he was spiralling out of control and enough was enough.

He got on with a construction crew and vowed to stay one year. He discovered that he handled tools well and liked the logic of the work: you measured, you cut, and if it didn't fit you fixed it, and did a better job the next time. It was solid and tangible and not without beauty. His growing competency made him feel better about himself. He liked the clean smell of fir in the cool of the morning, and the spice of sap beading on the two-by-fours in the heat of the afternoon; he even liked the scent of asphalt shingles and the smell of wet cement. Before long a load of lumber was a house, each house was distinct, and every few months you moved on.

Even on the job he found time to sketch. Whenever he had a moment—and often when he didn't have a moment because he should have been working—he'd sharpen one of his wide flat carpenter's pencils and draw vines climbing the two-by-four uprights of a doorframe, embellishing them with leaves in which lurked naked elf maids with come hither eyes. The rest of the crew would discover them and follow the scenes unscrolling lewdly along window frames and across joists as though watching an animated film that rewarded their diligence with tits here, ass there, occasionally even a bit of bestiality. Drawing on wood presented its own unique challenges, and he was always pleased when he could incorporate the knots and woodgrain into his images: the grain as flowing hair, a knot as an orifice. He became a great favourite with his fellow workers, though they'd howl with disappointment and beat the floor with their hammers if Cyril failed to provide them with a penultimate scene from the *kama sutra* or some satisfying vision of girl-on-girl.

The foreman indulged this behaviour until one afternoon the owner arrived unexpectedly and toured his home-to-be and, baulking at the pornographic graffiti desecrating what would one day be his child's bedroom, demanded it be sanded off.

∽ ∾

"You should quit," said Gilbert.

"And do what?"

"Come to San Francisco with me and get some of that free love. You could do graffiti. Or T-shirts. Or body painting. All those hippie chicks want their tits painted."

While there was a definite allure to painting boobs, Cyril didn't want to go to San Francisco, he wanted to go to Los Angeles, because he'd received a letter from Connie.

Dear C,

First of all, apologies for not writing.
I'm a total s—t. No excuses but lots of
explanations. Like working two jobs
and going to auditions and rehearsals.
Hardly time to breathe. The competition's
fierce. And to be honest there isn't much
call for my type here if you get my drift.
Though did have a role in an episode

of I Spy. *Got to use a gun. Cosby and*
Culp are so cool. It was a taste. Amazing
how long you can live on a taste.
I meant to write sooner. But the thing is
you'd write back, (I hope), then I'd miss
you so much I might come running home,
and I might end up resentful. Not fair to
you or me. It was cold turkey or nothing.
I hope you understand that. (It's a compliment.)
So what're you doing with yourself? Married?
Kids? Teaching art? Doing art? Stealing art?
Let me know. And if you're ever passing
through L.A. drop in on us. If you don't
and I find out you're dead.
Hope this wasn't too out of the blue.

Love,
C

He'd reread the letter so many times he could recite it like a poem. But for all the sweet sentiment it all came down to one troubling word. *Us.* Drop in on *us.* No mention of her being married, no mention of a boyfriend, but there was that word, *us.* He'd have gone to Los Angeles in a minute if not for that one small word, those two tiny letters. He tried reinterpreting the letter, wondering if there was any way *us* might mean just her? Did it refer to Hollywood in general, to the city as a whole, was she perhaps identifying so completely with the place that she had become plural, or was it the sort of thing that happened to actors who had, he assumed, multiple characters to choose from for their various roles? Or had she inserted that one little word as a caution? It occurred to him to simply write and ask, except he couldn't bear the truth even after four years. *Us* meant *us*. She was a couple.

Which meant Los Angeles was out. Gilbert drove a lot of Americans in his cab and heard non-stop stories about sex and drugs. It was 1966 and the ever curious Gilbert acquired some LSD, and one Sunday at the beach he made a performance of cutting a confetti-sized square of paper in two then piercing one half on the tip of his Swiss Army knife.

"Behold." Gilbert's hair hung to his collarbones and he sported motorcycle shades and a Joe Namath Fu Manchu moustache that was impressively thick and black. He licked the flake of paper from the blade tip then pierced the other half and offered it to Cyril. "Don't want to hit the Haight as LSD virgins. We gotta be experienced."

Cyril glanced around. They were at Spanish Banks, the beach crowded with families, couples, sunbathing girls, screaming kids, seniors in sling chairs. He wondered if Connie had tried LSD. He knew Paul certainly hadn't. Paul thought hippies should be sent to coal mines or Vietnam. Yet colours and shapes were said to take on new life. Baudelaire took opium and he had no doubt that Salvadore Dali had as well. Maybe he'd finally understand what was up with the flies and honey. He pinched the half hit of acid from the knife-tip and swallowed it down.

"Bravo, my friend."

"Now what?"

"We wait."

"How long?"

"Until we're there."

"Where's there?"

"Right here."

Lying on the sand, Cyril's heart sped. It was noon, the sun gold in an azure sky. By half past twelve he felt nothing, by one he felt nothing, by half past one he realised that Gilbert had played a joke on him, and while he was relieved he was also disappointed. By two he was sitting up cross-legged pouring the miracle of sand from one hand to the other. How was it that sand could be melted down into glass, and how was it that something as solid as glass could be transparent? He stretched himself out on the hot sand and began to writhe, discovering the delicious feel of the sand against his skin. Oblivious of anyone watching, he writhed slowly to get the full satisfaction. Then he sat up. Gilbert was petting a log as though it was a cat.

"This log is a genius," said Gilbert.

Cyril understood. They knelt side-by-side.

"Ask it anything. Go on. It's an oracle."

Cyril had no questions. Life was all too perfectly clear for questions. Electricity, radio waves, space, even glass, all made sense. He petted the log.

"It's purring," said Gilbert.

Cyril put his ear to the sun-bleached driftwood and discovered that it was, like a great big cat, a panther, a puma, a leopard.

They remained with their ears to the wood and then convulsed in laughter.

"Swim," said Gilbert, sending the word like a smoke ring into the air.

Before he reached the water Cyril dropped to the damp corrugated low tide sand and began drawing, trembling at the electric sensation on his fingertips, listening to the delicate scraping sound, intrigued by the texture of the lines and savouring the scent of brine. He thought of sea caves and galleons, the particulate existence of grit.

He raised his hand and began drawing on the air with his finger. Contrails of colour hung before his eyes and he spread his fingers in wondering admiration then began drawing with all ten fingers at once, each one independent and yet each one orchestrated with the others. A spider. A puppet master. He saw cinematic tapestries flowing in time lapse speed from his fingertips: Hieronymus Bosch, the Mouseketeers, Muhammad Ali, the earth itself rotating with its coastlines and mountain ranges beneath a living gauze of cloud.

Then they were bombing along the beach road in Gilbert's Bug with the surface of the world flowing over them. Up ahead an owl dropped from the trees and plucked a rat from a ditch. It was so swift, so perfectly executed, that Cyril thought it must have been rehearsed, that it was a scene from a movie, that they were not driving at all but sitting in a theatre, or perhaps—and this sucked the breath right out of him—*in* a movie, and that therein lay the secret of secrets, that God was Otto Preminger in a beret with a cigarette in a holder clenched between his teeth.

Gilbert skidded to a halt. He turned to Cyril and stated solemnly, as though declaring a long-meditated decision to renounce the world and join a monastery, that he wanted to be a bird.

Cyril shattered in laughter.

Gilbert shoved the Bug in gear and drove on. "I *am* a bird."

Cyril spread his arms, the right one out the window feeling the wind, the left reaching into the back seat. They passed a stone church and Gilbert looped the block like a hawk banking to come in behind its prey. As they entered the familiar gloom, Gilbert said, "I'm leaving my soul to science."

Cyril envisioned lab-coated doctors dissecting the mist that was Gilbert's soul.

They each took an aisle, Gilbert traveling on down the left, Cyril the right, leaving the middle open to a black scarfed woman kneeling at the altar where candles burned on a tiered iron rack like a silent choir of small spirits. A stained glass crucifixion throbbed in the evening sunlight. The cool cement floor chilled Cyril's bare feet. He envisioned Roman soldiers tramping the hard dry roads of Palestine. Opening his eyes, he saw Christ gazing at him from an alcove. One of Christ's eyes flickered, as if winking at him, then it rose into the air— Christ's eye was taking flight! Cyril staggered. Reaching for balance he grabbed the statue's ankle, hollow plaster instead of solid concrete, and it toppled, grazing his shoulder and striking the cement floor. Christ's head snapped off at the neck and rocked side to side and then was still, while the moth Cyril had mistaken for an eye flew off toward the candles.

Cyril woke before dawn. He hadn't been sleeping so much as awake and dreaming. Now he was shivering and thirsty. He drank from the tap and then went outside and stood listening to the idling machinery of the city. The eastern sky was turning apple green by the time he reached his mother's. He entered the dark basement and did not turn on the light because he knew that his father was there waiting for him and that in the light he would vanish.

"Cyril."

"Dad."

"I'm glad you're here."

"Me too."

"You're grown up."

Cyril wanted to say not really, that he was still a child, that they could pick up where they'd left off. His father appeared luminous and yet solid. There was a hiss of gas and the scrape of a rasp-lighter and the welding torch spouted its perfect flame. His dad flipped down his face plate and went to work cutting a door in the darkness. He worked his way slowly up one side and across and then down the other with his blue and gold flame as precise as a knife blade. A doorway dropped open like a drawbridge revealing a field of wheat higher than their heads. His father switched off the torch and turned off the valve then flipped up his face plate and hung it on its nail. He stepped through the door from the darkness to the light. The sky was a deep blue and a breeze combed the wheat.

"Don't go, dad."

"Come."

They entered the wheat that smelled of wet grain and hot sun.

"How far?"

"All the way."

Cyril followed. His father was in overalls with the sleeves pushed to mid-forearm. They moved soundlessly, the wheat stalks flowing past, his father singing slowly, quietly, then louder, in a voice deep and resonant as if rising right up out of the land itself, the land he was born in and had returned to, with its winds that blew across thousands of miles of tilled fields and through birch forests, and even though his dad sang no words, only notes, Cyril understood—

"Cyril." The basement light went on, the bare bulb's brutal glare obliterating the vision to reveal his mother on the stairs in her housecoat.

✧ ✧

He worked on a letter to Connie, achieving a pile of crumpled paper and two words:

Dear Connie,

Too formal. He crossed out *Dear* and in a burst he wrote:

Hey Connie, great to hear from you.

He pondered then replaced the period with an exclamation mark.

I Spy! *That's great. I love* I Spy.

This was true. He especially enjoyed the theme music and the opening credits that showed a silhouette of Robert Culp—undercover CIA agent Kelly Robinson—playing tennis, backhand, forehand, then pivoting with a pistol and blasting some Russian or Albanian as the names of exotic cities slid past: Moscow, Rome, Beirut.

Where does your episode take place? It's great you're doing so well.

Rereading what he had so far, he discovered that he'd repeated the word *great* three times. Clunky. He tapped his pencil on the lined letter paper.

I finished art school and just had my first solo show and sold everything.

He contemplated, then added,

I'm moving to New York. Get there much?

He reversed the pencil about to erase it all then changed his mind and laid the pencil down, discovering that the very act of letting the lie stand for a minute was an exhilarating act of bravado. Two days the letter remained on the table. During those two days Cyril's moods churned. He felt guilty, he felt silly, and then he became critical of Connie—not harshly, but gently, as if he was older and wiser—and thought she could benefit from his example by proceeding more slowly with her career. Was she taking acting classes or blindly hurling herself into auditions and blowing opportunities?

On the third day he came home from work with the staccato echo of hammers in his head to find Gilbert at the table, a Lucky in one hand, the letter in the other. He'd shifted the tube-metal chair so that he sat parallel to the table, his legs crossed at the knees, looking the picture of comfort.

"If you're still carrying a torch for her you should go to LA."

"She's with someone."

Gilbert popped the cap from a beer with the opener on his Swiss Army knife and slid the bottle across the Formica.

Cyril drank deeply.

"So why are you suddenly writing her? You think these fantasies about shows and New York will what, bring her running?"

"I was drunk."

"A little bullshit can go a long way," admitted Gilbert.

"I wasn't going to send it."

"Maybe you should."

"Send it?"

"Go to New York." Gilbert swirled his beer and looked at the sketches tacked to the walls, portraits, landscapes, houses, body parts, bottles, boxes, bugs, forks and spoons and knives. "Anything and everything," he said. "You need to focus. You have no direction. You need a teacher. A mentor. Isn't that how it worked in the old days, you apprenticed, mixed the master's paints, shined his shoes, stretched his canvases?"

SIX

FEARING THAT AT the grand old age of twenty-three he was too old to return to school, even if it was only night school, where all you had to do was pay your tuition to be admitted, Cyril was relieved to see students of all ages. They were mostly women, about a dozen, some in smocks with kerchiefs around their heads, others with elbow length hair and hoop earrings. The instructor was named Sandor Novak. His damp hair and dark eyes drooped like his moustache, and he moved with slow slapping steps as though his feet were flat and ankles weak. He showed them his own work, which focused almost entirely on dismembered dolls. He'd set their heads like boulders in bleak seascapes with crab claws and screwdrivers and broken rowboats and rat skulls. A doll's foot, a doll's butt, a doll's eyes large and lidless, each rendered with detail verging on the mad. Many students exchanged sceptical glances. Cyril was excited. The juxtapositions of such strange and diverse subject matter was a revelation: suddenly everything had aesthetic potential.

Over the following weeks, Novak put the class through exercises where they drew with their eyes closed, with their opposite hand, where they drew whatever they were looking at as though it was upside down or imagined it from the opposite side.

"They say some dinosaurs had two brains," said Novak. "One up here." He touched his temple. "And one in their tails." He held up his hand. "Let us develop a brain in our hand."

Novak brought in models. Rarely were they beautiful. There was a scarred and fat old man with a long beard, a withered female junkie who shivered and scratched, a body builder, an elderly woman who fell asleep, a native woman with beaded hair to her hips and who, afterwards, strolled behind them in a black and red robe inspecting their work. She paused behind Cyril and stood there for what seemed an eternity.

"Huh." Then she moved on.

He evaluated that *huh*. It was not a *harumph*, or a sceptical *hunh*, but a bemused and perhaps even intrigued sound. He had focused on the drapery of her hair as if it was a theatre curtain.

When Novak looked at Cyril's sketch he did not say *Huh* he sucked his teeth. "Well, you know which end of the pencil to use." Cyril was familiar enough with Eastern European bluntness to know that while it was not exactly a compliment neither was it a complete dismissal. "You are drawing what you think is there not what *is* there. I'll give you a trick. If your drawing is going well you don't need it. But if you're stuck, this can help. Look for images. You understand? Maybe you look at our lovely madonna of the forest and you see that where her arm meets her shoulder there is a chicken."

"Not the chickens again," she said, overhearing.

Novak ignored her and spoke louder. "A chicken. Or tree. Or boot. You draw that chicken or tree or boot and in that way you build up the whole from the parts, and each part is its own shape."

Cyril discovered that his drawings began taking on what Novak termed interior architecture. He was excited. He began imagining a route forward, maybe even a show, a career. Yet why did a guy with Novak's talent have to teach? One evening he asked whether Novak could make a living on his art.

"Ah, the honourable sir has enquired if I, Novak, could survive on the avails of my art alone. I could. But I choose not to. Why? Because I do not wish to become a bitter and loathsome creature. I prefer to remain the sweet boy you see before you now." His mock beatific expression fell. He frowned. He had many frowns. He could frown musingly, sourly, angrily, whimsically, sadly, even joyously. He could laugh and frown at the same time. Now he frowned reflectively. "You must have talent. A thick skin. And, most important, luck. Luck, luck, luck. So much luck. To make luck you must be clever, or blessed. I know I am not blessed and I suspect I am not so clever, but I believe I have the sweet sad soul of a melted popsicle."

Cyril had no idea what any of that meant, but he was inspired.

∽ ∾

Sunday evenings Cyril visited his mother. Paul and Della would be there, and after helping with the dishes Della would dry her hands and inevitably discover her wristwatch and remember how early she had to get up in the morning and they'd escape, leaving Cyril and his mother to Ed Sullivan. She didn't watch the *Ed Sullivan Show* so much as gaze at it the way she looked at the cemetery, with a distant and somewhat disdainful curiosity. She regarded José Feliciano as doubly handicapped because he was both blind *and* Puerto Rican. She liked Liberace's sequinned outfits and rhinestone rings, though Victor Borge was her favourite because he'd made fun of Hitler in the '30s.

She had developed the gravity of a brick. There was some latent danger in her that put Cyril in mind of an unexploded shell that had sat buried for decades. It might go years more or blow within the hour. He knew she had friends, other widows from church, yet he feared that by driving Darrel off he'd condemned her to misery.

At the next class Cyril spent as much time looking at Novak as he did at the model, evaluating Novak through his mother's eyes: the narrow shoulders, the slack hair, the flat feet, the sarcasm—a quality they shared—and the fact that they were from the same end of Europe. Of course, Novak was blithely irreverent when it came to religion while Cyril's mother attended church and took more and more solace in her icons. There was also the little matter of him being Hungarian. They'd fought, however reluctantly, alongside Germany in the war. No, his mother and Novak were not a good match. But wasn't that for them to decide?

At first Novak didn't understand. "A party?"

"Supper."

Novak pushed his lips up under his long nose and asked after Cyril's father, and learning that he was dead began getting the idea. He frowned his exaggerated frown, each end of his thin-lipped mouth hooking downwards and his coat-hanger shoulders rising in a shrug. "Okay."

At first Cyril's mother was equally sceptical. "Magyar."

"Canadian."

"Magyar."

"So?"

She regarded him with horror. "They fought alongside the Germans."

"Dad fought with the Commies."

"They think they're—" Her hand flapped like a torn flag. "They think they're better."

"He's a good guy."

She sniffed as only she could sniff, nostrils wide, mouth down, implying disinterest and disdain. "Bring him, don't bring him."

Come Sunday the bright blue skirt and yellow blouse and red lipstick and cornflower clip-on earrings said Helen Andrachuk was not so indifferent. On the dining room table were new cloth napkins with red trim, and from the kitchen came the smell of roast pork and apple sauce. Paul and Della were eager to meet this Novak. Dinner was at six. At a quarter to seven Novak still hadn't shown and Paul, deep into the rye, said the guy must be on Budapest time. At seven o'clock Novak arrived carrying a large bottle of Hungarian red whose label depicted some sort of medieval wood furnace being fed by trolls. He was smartly dressed in a charcoal suit and open-collared cream shirt.

Paul said, "You're late."

"I missed the bus."

"You don't drive?'

"I drive when I have a car." Novak turned and waited to be introduced to Cyril's mother, taking her hand in both of his and regarding her with a decorum nothing short of courtly. Cyril could see by her expression that she was charmed by such graciously Old World manners. When it was Della's turn Novak asked if she would model for him.

"No," said Paul.

Della, angered, said she'd love to.

Paul, angered, said she wouldn't.

Novak, amused, asked if Paul would like to model and Della said he'd love to.

Paul gulped his rye in one go and said he was hungry and took his spot at the head of the table. Cyril saw Novak discovering the collection of Virgin Marys as well as the view out the window of the cemetery. Cyril offered to close the curtains but Novak said no, it was a very entertaining vista.

"It's depressing," said Paul, filling their glasses with red wine.

"It makes you remember to live," said Novak, raising his glass toward his hostess and thanking her. She said he was vel—*wel*come.

As Paul carved the glistening slab of pork, he asked if Novak was one of those guys who sat in Stanley Park on Sunday doing sketches. Novak said he was very flattered that Paul might think so but no, he was not, though maybe someday he might aspire to such heights. Failing to get a rise, Paul wondered how many Viet Cong the Americans had knocked off today?

"They say eleven," said Novak. "Which probably means two."

"Too bad," she said. Communists of any race or colour were

to be crushed like cockroaches. "How long you have—*have you*—been in Canada?" asked Cyril's mother.

"Since '55. The year before the Soviets paid us their little visit. I saw the tanks on the horizon and went the other way."

"A country built on tanks and barbed wire," said Paul, serving the roast. "And run by pigs."

"The pig is an admirable beast," said Novak through a mouthful of pork. "Smart. A survivor."

"Not this one," said Paul, spearing a piece of meat.

"I prefer the horse," said Cyril's mother.

This came as a surprise. She'd never expressed any interest in horses or any other animal, except to complain about the crows which haunted the cemetery and cawed raucously each morning and evening.

Novak agreed that horses were a fine and noble creature, and described once seeing a horse trotting across the *Széchenyi Lánchíd*—the Chain Bridge—in Budapest during the war. "It had lost its rider but his boots—tall shiny black boots—were both still in the stirrups."

"The pigs got him," said Paul, happily.

"One can only hope," said Novak. He raised his glass and they drank to the pig.

Cyril studied the table. Della, a third generation Canadian of English-Scottish heritage, had long given up trying to fathom the medieval animosities that shaped her husband's background. Paul, in spite of every intention otherwise, seemed to be warming to Novak, while their mother, Helen, was studying their guest with a wine-fueled glimmer in her eyes. Cyril envisioned life with Novak as his stepfather. Would his mother discover a respect for the arts, and in so doing a respect for Cyril's own efforts? Would Novak become Cyril's mentor? Or would Novak and his mother fight, divorce, and Novak walk off with half the house? The guy didn't even own a car. Had Cyril invited the wolf in the door?

Soon they moved on to Novak's bottle of red. Paul asked what Novak did in the war and Novak gave his shrug and frown and said he was a mouse. "I lived in walls, in basements, in closets, sometimes in the sewer, though mostly in attics. The Russians—and their pals the Ukrainians and Romanians—they didn't like going up stairs. Too lazy. And you never know what is waiting for you. We came down after dark for the midnight buffet of frozen horse. Mwa!" He kissed his fingers. "And if the dogs or rats beat us to it we broke the teeth from the horses and ground them in a mortar and pestle and drank the powder in melted snow. Very high in calcium."

"Ukraine had no choice."

"*Au contraire*, madame," said Novak, "we all had plenty of choice. The choice to be shot by the Germans or shot by the Russians or to shoot ourselves. And since so few of us had the grace for the latter, most of us obeyed."

Cyril, aware that his father had participated in the Siege of Budapest, watched the faces of his mother and Paul.

"Not that there wasn't a certain dark joy on the part of everyone seeing Hungary carved like this roast and served out to Romanians," said Novak. "Romanians." He pushed his plate away as if nauseated. "People who don't even know which end of the goat to fuck."

Cyril's mother threw down her napkin; Della's eyes were wide and fearful; Paul was happy, as though the real entertainment was finally beginning.

"Ukraine got nothing."

"My Lady, other than to be left alone Ukraine deserved nothing." Novak finished his wine, dabbed his mouth with his napkin, stood and bowed to her. "An excellent dinner and a most enchanting evening." He turned. "You should really consider modeling," he said to Della. "And you young sir." He extended his hand to Paul who, not knowing what else to do, shook it. "Interesting to meet you." To Cyril he said, "Wednesday." And showed himself out.

No one spoke for a full minute. Then, with bitterness and bewilderment, Cyril's mother asked, "You couldn't do better than him?"

ᔄ ᔅ

The next class Cyril expected some sardonic remark from Novak but there was nothing, instead he announced that it was time for a show. Everyone assumed he meant they should gather around to look at his latest work, or some comic pantomime that he'd cooked up, but he meant theirs. "The time has come, my babies. The time has come."

Fear rocked the class like a quake followed by aftershocks of delight and confusion. Cyril clung to his easel riding out the tremor.

"I have reserved the school gallery," said Novak, standing on the models' dais. "For one week you will have your fifteen minutes." Novak gazed at each of them, the solemnity of his look like a hand pressed on their shoulders in a final reassurance before sending them up and out of the trench and into the battle. Did Novak's gaze rest a little longer on Cyril? They'd never spoken of it, but Cyril believed he was Novak's favourite, the one with the potential, the one of whom he expected the most, the real artist among the amateurs, and the show would prove it. Admittedly, the competition was not intense. At least one student a semester took the class only because it fit their schedule, or because Tagalog or *feng shui* or flower arranging were full, a fact Novak accepted with impressive serenity, as if such humiliation were his due.

The show was titled *The Figure in Fact and Fancy*. Novak spoke an adventurous English, and was pleased with the alliteration. He had considered calling it *Ass and Tits*, yet Cyril and the others advised caution. The class did a poster that showed a crowd of human figures resembling tall grass sprouting from the back of a grinning toad. Cyril drew the toad; Novak was delighted with the poster. An ad ran in the college newsletter, in *The Georgia Straight*, and the arts page of *The Sun*. The opening took place on a Thursday evening in April. All were welcome.

Helen was not enthused about being in the same room as Novak again but Paul looked forward to being in the same room as a lot of naked women, even if they were only on the walls.

Cyril turned his drawings upside down and on their sides, examining his work from every angle. Did he dare call it "his work?" Certainly it involved his labour, but "his work" carried connotations implying a dizzying level of confidence and commitment. He avoided the issue by sticking to the word "drawings" instead.

Novak had encouraged them to put prices on their pictures. Cyril suspected that his mother's reaction, as well as Paul and

Gilbert's, would depend entirely on sales, for sales equalled success while no sales equalled flop. Yet he couldn't price them so low as to be virtually giving them away. A hundred dollars each? Would he pay a hundred for one of his own drawings? Would he pay fifty? He compromised at seventy-five. Then there was the issue of frames and glass, which meant jacking the prices back up to one hundred. A hundred was a nice round solid number suggesting concrete self-assurance on the part of the artist—though was he an artist or only some guy who drew?

Things got off to a bad start when the previous exhibition—*A History of Wax*—was not cleared from the gallery until just two hours before the opening. While Novak shouted at the balding candle-maker with the ponytail, Cyril and the others raced to hang their work, their *pictures*, amid the lingering scent of beeswax.

The show opened at 7:00 PM and by 8:00 there were only twenty-three people, eleven of them the artists themselves, twelve if you included Novak. It peaked at 9:00 with forty, forty-one if you included the janitor who had stepped in leaving his mop and bucket in the corridor. When Novak saw Cyril's mother he insisted on taking her arm and touring her through the gallery, expansively acknowledging the virtues of every piece on the walls. She looked at Novak as if he was a talking cat, simultaneously intrigued and appalled. When it came to Cyril's pictures he was especially effusive. His mother sucked her teeth and regarded the line drawings of fat naked men and skinny naked women. Her experience of art had been the blunt brutalities of Russian Formalism: smoke stacks, hammers and anvils, the fists and forearms of burly men, the sweaty breasts of bullock-shaped women. She began to weep. Novak opened his arms wide and embraced her and for a moment the two of them sobbed together while Cyril and Paul and Della and Gilbert stared. Then their mother shoved Novak away, sniffed once, elevated her chin and resumed her tour of the gallery alone, a solitary ship at sea.

Only half the students showed up for the next class. Cyril presumed they were home sobbing in their rooms or hiding under their beds, or plotting revenge for the review that had appeared.

While the work cannot be criticized for being what it is, that is to say amateurish, it can be criticized for being displayed. All the more so for being displayed in a gallery subsidized by taxpayer dollars.

"Jesus Christ," said Gilbert, reading the review aloud to Cyril in case he'd missed it.

Cyril, scalded, feigned indifference.

"We should find this bastard," said Gilbert, whose tone of sincere concern could not mask a hint of sheer delight.

Cyril understood. He hated him but he understood.

"What did what's his nuts say?" asked Gilbert, meaning Novak.

"Fail better next time."

PART TWO – 1972

In Which the Match Burns Twice

ONE

SITTING IN THE BEER parlour of the Europe Hotel before his drawing session one evening, Cyril paged through *The Province*. It had been a lively spring. Howard Hughes was holed up in the Bayshore Inn, George Chuvalo had gone twelve rounds with Muhammad Ali right here at the Coliseum, and Novak's buddy Elek Imredy had unveiled his statue *Girl in a Wetsuit* on a rock off Stanley Park. Cyril was intrigued by the hermit billionaire, admired the indomitable Chuvalo, and wondered if the statue shouldn't have been holding an umbrella given its perpetual smear of seagull droppings.

Cyril had discovered that two beers went down well before class. He grew relaxed yet not sloppy, adventurous yet not irreverent. He reached the Entertainment Section and spotted an ad for a live theatre version of *The World of Suzie Wong*. The West Bay Theatre Troupe of San Francisco was touring and Connie Chow had the starring role.

"You want front row?" The clerk showed him a laminated card depicting the seating plan.

Cyril didn't want front row, he wanted to hide as far back in the shadows as possible, yet be close enough to see everything. He pointed to the last row in the Lower Orchestra. "How about here?"

He arrived early and drank two beers in the carpeted lobby. It was an older crowd, well-dressed, lots of jewelry and perfume, the conversations murmured and polite. He was wearing a black turtleneck sweater and black jeans. He'd filled out, having grown broad across the chest and shoulders due to his carpentry work. He had thick dark sideburns as well as a blackened thumbnail where he'd been whacked by a board. The last time he'd been to the theatre was in high school when Connie was in *A Midsummer Night's Dream*. That audience had smelled of B.O. and bubblegum; this one smelled of dry cleaning and cigarettes. He was twenty-seven, ten years had passed since he'd seen her. These numbers stuck like poisoned darts and a bewildered confusion seeped through him: confusion at how quickly the years had passed and bewilderment that he'd let it happen while accomplishing so little. Each time he took up a pencil—never as often as he should—it seemed his fingers had thickened and he had a new blood blister. And there was the fact that Connie had not called, and he'd learned about the performance by accident.

He'd responded to her first letter in truthful if enigmatic blandness: *Hey Connie, good to hear form you. Glad you're doing so well. I love* I Spy! *I wish you all the best and hope to see you sometime. (No, not stealing any art but I am doing a lot of drawing.)* She'd sent him three postcards since, including one of a famous hot dog stand in the shape of a hot dog, the Eiffel Tower from a European tour, and the Statue of Liberty from her time in New York in an off-Broadway show. He'd responded to each. A postcard of Lumberman's Arch, one of Lions Gate Bridge all lit up at night, and one of the fat neon figure of The Smilin' Buddha. The word *us* did not appear in any of her cards, though one did mention her and someone called Guillermo going to Mexico City. Cyril felt compelled to mention how he and Jaclyn had been to Seattle and gone up the Space Needle. It wasn't much but it was the best he could do. Jaclyn was a sweet and attractive and sensual girl. They might have lasted longer than one summer—she liked to dance naked while wearing his carpenter's belt—but she'd been obsessed with the word *get*. She'd wanted Cyril to *get* serious and *get* his shit together, and *get* his own business going so they could *get* married and *get* a house and *get* on with having a family. His mother thought she was a good influence.

A discrete bell ushered them to their seats. Cyril followed the crowd into the Lower Orchestra and discovered he had the row to himself. Would she spot him? Again he felt stung at not having heard from her now of all times. The bell tinged once more and the patrons settled themselves. Cyril couldn't have been more anxious if he was going on stage himself. As the lights went down he slid lower in his seat and held his breath. Bar music. The clamour of drunks. Then red lights went up and there she was, jiving with a sailor in a hazy Hong Kong tavern. To one side, Robert Lomax, the aspiring painter, sips a beer and admires her as she dances. He wears a suit, smokes a cigarette, and has hair as slick and shiny as an oiled LP. Suzie wears a high-collared knee-length dress of tight white silk, her hair long and loose. Watching in envy and admiration, Cyril tasted orange on his lips and vowed right there in the theatre to work harder at his drawing, but it wasn't just that, it was trickier than mere labour, it was taking himself and his drawing—his art, his work—more seriously. Isn't that what Connie had done? Is that not why she was on stage and he was in the audience?

During intermission he stepped outside into the cool clear night and listened to the city racket around him. There'd been a moment when he was sure she'd recognized him. She was alone on stage addressing the audience, her gaze travelling from side-to-side as if appealing to each individual about her fate. When her gaze crossed Cyril it seemed to stagger and made her speech stutter. Or had he imagined it? He went back in and had another beer and asked the bartender for a pen and wrote his name and number on a napkin. Approaching the Manager's door he hesitated then knocked. It opened instantly upon a cozy group that ceased talking and stared. A goateed man in a gold bow tie and owlish glasses waited for him to state his business.

"Could I leave this for Connie Chow?"

The man considered the folded napkin. He appeared amused and disdainful and considerate all at the same time. In a tone both reassuring and condescending he said, "I'll see that she gets it."

Back in his seat he reminded himself that she was probably busy, that there were only two performances and then they were off to Winnipeg. He wondered about her leading man. How could they go through this night after night, travelling together, staying in the same hotels, with nothing developing between them? He regretted leaving a lousy napkin, it should have been a card, something better, something sophisticated.

Connie looked good; she looked great, and no longer needed oranges in her brassiere.

After the final curtain the actors came out for an ovation, Connie and her leading man taking centre stage, holding hands and bowing deeply. She smiled and blew kisses and the applause swelled and there were whistles, Cyril standing along with everyone else and clapping. Finally the celebration ebbed and people began moving to the aisles. Should he wait in the lobby? Wait until she called? And if she didn't call? The tidal current of the audience carried him outside leaving him beached on a sidewalk by a maple in a concrete tub. He looked back to where a few people lingered; he looked ahead to where taxis were pulling away. Had she groaned when she saw the note? Did the other actors roll their eyes in commiseration? He shoved his hands in his pockets and started across the street.

"What, you're just gonna leave?"

He turned and saw her walking toward him as if emerging from some tunnel utterly different and utterly the same as the last time he'd seen her. "I thought you'd be signing autographs," he said.

"I was. How the hell are you, man? Come on, get in here." She opened her arms and they hugged. She was wearing a black leather jacket with studs and chains, a black toque, and Daytons. The leather was fragrant. Or was that her? They stood apart, holding hands, appraising each other. She looked solid and confident and had silver rings on all her fingers including her thumbs.

"You ride?"

"Five hundred Kawi," she said.

"Got time for a drink?"

"Well, duh."

They walked to the *Alcazar* and found a table near the fountain. Her hair was tied in a thick braid and her black t-shirt said Fart, parodying the *Ford* logo.

"I don't see a ring," she said, indicating his bare finger.

"What about you?" he asked.

She splayed her fingers, admiring all the silver, then told him about Guillermo, a metals speculator from Bolivia who liked to play around and did most of his apologizing to her in silver jewelry. "When I finally ran out of fingers I figured it was time to leave him."

He asked her about children and she said she didn't think she was the mothering type.

"You're doing what you always wanted," he said.

She looked at her beer and shrugged, all bravado momentarily lapsing. Then she brightened. "Met Nancy Kwan. She came to the premiere. Did a few *Hawaii Five-Os. The Mod Squad. Green Hornet.* Had a part this big in *The Happening* with Faye Dunaway and Anthony Quinn." She held her thumb and forefinger a quarter an inch apart. "Lots of small bits. Crumbs."

"And *I Spy*," he said.

"Yeah, that was cool."

"So you're surviving."

"Just."

He was impressed and he was envious and he was resentful and he could, with only the slightest encouragement, fall right back in love with her.

"You drawing?"

"Sure. Some. Never enough." He mentioned Sandor Novak

and the drawing classes though omitted the disastrous art show.

"Sandor, now that's a great name," she said. "If I had a cat I'd name it Sandor."

He felt compelled in the interest of honesty to mention the framing crew.

"That's cool. It's solid. Real. I like that." Her excess enthusiasm was awkwardly obvious to them both. "Hey, anything I ever said before, you know, about what you are or will be, I mean what the fuck do I know, I can barely make my rent. You hungry?"

For a moment he thought she was referring to his level of ambition.

They headed to Pender Street for wonton, passing the *Marco Polo* where a man out front was doing tricks with a yo-yo for a small but appreciative crowd, and entered a restaurant featuring shiny red ducks dangling from hooks. They found a booth and took in the genial chaos of clattering bowls and chopsticks while fluorescent tubes crackled on the ceiling and dragons glared from the walls. For almost a full minute they said nothing and Cyril endured a stab of panic thinking that if he didn't come up with something good she'd get bored and find an excuse to escape, reducing him to just some guy she used to know who didn't have the talent or drive to escape the drizzly backwater of Vancouver. He plucked a menu from the metal rack and took refuge in the choices: Crispy Skin Duck, Five Spiced Duck, Fried Smoked Duck.

"How about Pork Stomach and Pork Blood with Chives?" Connie suggested.

"Great."

"Cyril." She stuck her finger down her throat.

"You're cruel and unusual."

She batted her eyelashes. "So sweet of you to say."

A waitress scuffed over and flipped open her order pad like an angry cop ready to write a ticket. Her custard-coloured uniform was grease stained and her name tag said Grace. "Ready order?"

"How's about we go for the plain old Szechuan Duck, some rice, a plate of bok choy, and a couple of deep-fried bad-for-your-cholesterol egg rolls. You got beer?"

"Tsing tao."

Connie glanced at Cyril. "Two?"

He was desperately thirsty and not above taking refuge in booze. "Make it four."

"Right on," growled Connie. "Give us four." The waitress scuffed off toward the kitchen. Connie slotted the menu into the rack and then groaned and leaned her head in her hands. "I am so beat. But hey—" Her head popped up. "It's so good to see you, man. I tried giving you a call. Or maybe I didn't. I meant to. Honest. I think about you a lot. You were the only friend I had."

He was flattered and hopeful and embarrassed. "You vanished," he said.

She became apologetic. "I do that. It's shitty. I do a lot of shitty things. I don't know. I couldn't handle it."

This came as a shock. Connie Chow unable to cope?

"Hot in here." She plucked the toque from her head and fanned herself.

The waitress passed with something orange and gelatinous quivering atop something grey and gelatinous.

"Hey, you still chew *Black Cat*?" he asked.

"*Black Cat*. God. I could use some *Black Cat* gum. That's what my life's been missing. I'm gonna buy like fifty packs."

When their food arrived they dug in and soon their lips were shiny. At one point she broke into a drum solo on the tabletop with her chopsticks and said she'd been in a band but was the shits so quit.

Afterwards, they walked up the street to an old hotel, three storeys, narrow and deep and weathered. "Trying to keep the Hong Kong mood going," she explained. "Wanna come up?" They climbed two flights of spongy grey linoleum steps into the smell of decades-old dirt and stale air. An old man sat in a booth labouring over a crossword. "How's it going, Milt?"

"Four-letter-word for woman. Last three letters u-n-t."

Connie looked at Cyril who politely cleared his throat and declined to offer a suggestion. "How about aunt," said Connie.

Milt brightened. "That's it!" He turned his pencil and began furiously erasing. "Ha!"

They went down a hallway and she unlocked a door which sent pigeons clattering from the windowsill on the far side of the room. "Not much of a view," she said of the brick wall opposite. She shrugged off her jacket. There was a metal-framed bed, a sink, as well as a chair and table that didn't match. Snoring came from the next room; on the other side someone swearing drunkenly.

"Nice."

"I think the word is character."

"Where's the rest of the cast?"

"Motel 6. Budget's lean. The tour's a risk. Chair or bed?"

He sat on the ladder-back chair and she lay on the bed and

propped her head on her fist. He noted the pleasing swell of her hip. Little Connie Chow had most definitely filled out. She jutted her chin and said he looked sturdier than she remembered.

"And you look…impressive."

"Impressive?" She mulled that.

"Hollywood," he said.

"Please."

"You should be proud."

"You think so?"

He shrugged, suddenly feeling naive, and told her how in carpentry a nail with its head sticking up above the wood was said to be proud.

"All the better to get whacked down," she said darkly, prying off her Daytons which bumped like bricks to the floor.

Cyril looked around the room noting the wainscotting, the lumpy lath-and-plaster, the exposed pipes, the lino that curled against the walls. "This place looks like the real thing."

"1890. Ghosts coming out of the walls and everything. One looks like my granny."

Cyril had envied Connie having a grandmother who was so eccentric, although also wondered if the old woman was so fundamentally different from his own mother's grimly whimsical obsession with funerals and icons. "How is she?"

"The ghost?"

"Your grandmother."

"Met a man in the Lonely Hearts and moved to Montreal. I'll be seeing her in a couple of weeks."

He imagined Connie and her grandmother in some French café. He knew nothing of his own grandparents.

Lying back, Connie put her hands behind her head and yawned. "I am so thrashed."

Cyril looked at his watch. 1:35 AM. He stood.

"Sorry, I'm not very entertaining." She followed him into the hallway. "Good seeing you, man."

"You too."

They hugged. She was shorter without her boots and felt smaller without her leather, more the way he remembered her. He was about to suggest getting together tomorrow but she had her hand on the door ready to shut it. "Okay, see you."

As he passed the office Milt shouted, "Aunt!"

⌒ ⌒

He was still living in the top floor suite of the house with the downtown view. When he got home he stared out the window at the city and thought over the evening. She'd seemed genuinely pleased to see him, but he was here and she was there, and in another day she'd be gone, and what had he expected anyway? Nothing. Everything.

He stared at his latest drawings: boxes. He was drawing boxes. Not just any boxes: corrugated cardboard boxes. He thought of Connie looking at them and trying not to laugh. What the fuck was he doing drawing corrugated cardboard boxes? *Rarely have corrugated cardboard boxes been rendered with such loving attention to detail, with such passion. This reviewer will never look at corrugated cardboard boxes the same way again...* Still, they were good boxes, the folds so well rendered they invited you to run your finger along their edges. And the boxes had something else: the question of what was in them, what they contained, or perhaps more significantly what they hid. He thought of Gilbert's grandmother's wooden box with the pistol in it. Surely a box with a pistol in it looked different than a box containing a rose, or a box that was empty. Cyril sat down and worked on the latest box until the sun was rising and when Connie called at eleven he was in a dead sleep.

"You sleeping?"

"No. Well... sort of."

"What, you went out on the town after dumping me off?"

"I did some drawing."

"Of what?"

He looked at one of the boxes. Lies fast-forwarded through his mind. "Boxes."

"Boxes? Boxes of what?"

"Well, that's the thing, I'm figuring out what's in each one as I draw it."

There was a silence as she thought about this. "Cool."

"It might be empty," said Cyril, incapable of not undermining himself.

"Or there's a puppet inside," said Connie, jumping on the idea. "Or a clown. Clowns're so creepy."

"Or a sword jutting out from the inside," said Cyril, remembering her collection of swords.

"Yeah, yeah."

"Or fire," he said. "The box contains fire."

"Or a head. I'm thinking there's a head in it."

"Whose head?"

"Well, that's the whole mystery," she said, as though that was obvious.

They met outside her hotel where she was studying the

newspaper. "No review." She pitched the paper into a bin and shook her head.

Cyril assured her she'd been wonderful and she said be specific and he said her accent and she shrugged as if that was no great accomplishment, so he said she'd been compelling, and she said tell me more, and he said she was passionate and wholly convincing, and she said: "More." And he said she was heartbreaking, at which she smiled and said: "Please sir, more." And he said, "You sure did good rememberizing all them there lines, ma'am." And she said, "Thank you, I feel better."

They walked from Chinatown to the West End, then into Stanley Park and along the seawall. Dense white clouds tumbled across a hard blue sky while the low tide beach seethed with barnacles. A black lab bounded about the sand scattering gulls that fled screeling into the air while the owner shouted haplessly.

"So," Connie enquired with mock formality, "how's the family?"

He mentioned that Paul and Della now had twin sons, Chuckie and Steve, a pair of evil six-year-olds bent on household and eventually world domination, and that his mother was devoted to them. He did not mention how maddening it was seeing both his mother and Paul make a point of speaking Ukrainian to the twins, though there was some small grim satisfaction in the boys' refusal to learn.

"Is Paul still a runt?"

"A prosperous runt."

"Are the kids runts?"

Chuckie and Steve were big, thick-necked, round-shouldered thugs, Steve so light-fingered his pockets had to be checked every time he left a playmate's house; Chuckie, a bed-wetter, though each terrifyingly bright in a warped fashion, each habitual contrarians constantly fighting with each other and obsessed with winning arguments and delighting in proving Uncle Cyril wrong. He saw them at Sunday dinner each week where they regarded him with sneering scepticism. "They're galoots."

"Galoots," said Connie, enjoying the word. "That is some seriously fat pile of sulphur over there," she said of a massive pyramid of yellow on the North Shore. "I don't remember that."

"What's your first memory?"

"The sound of the Empress of India's horn as we were crossing the ocean. Yours?"

"The way the sheets in my bed had wrinkles and folds that cast shadows, and I could change them by tugging the sheet. It was like drawing, or sculpting."

She was looking at him wonderingly. "Huh. Actually, mine was puking up Cream of Wheat."

Cyril confessed that his was getting conked on the head by the ironing board that folded up into a closet on the wall.

They passed under the Lions Gate Bridge and eventually reached Third Beach where they sat on a log and watched the sun and clouds compete for control of the sky. A woman threw a stick for a dog which plunged splashing into the water. Another cheered and clapped and threw stick after stick for her dog yet it refused to get wet. The air was rich with brine and foliage, English Bay dense with freighters, and across the water the heights of West Van showed scraped patches of new housing developments like so much mange on a bear's back.

"Hey, Picasso."

Cyril saw Chantal, the bead-haired native model from his drawing class, walking arm-in-arm with Novak. Chantal gave a jaunty wave and Novak a courtly nod, and Cyril could see why Novak would choose her over his mother—if indeed she'd have had him—nonetheless he felt, even now, years later, indignant on her behalf.

Connie was impressed. "Aren't you cool."

The light fled across the water as a cloud slid over the sun. "So, do you have a date tonight?" he asked.

"Yeah, with Robert Lomax."

He smiled then gazed out at the changing sea. "I was thinking of after."

She regarded him as though looking through a window onto a room she was sceptical of entering. "That would be nice." She held out her hand and he took it and they sat in silence. He felt her hand gripping his tightly, like a child fearful of losing her balloon, and he was happy.

"You're not seeing anyone?" she asked, pointedly looking away to the left.

"Not really," he said, pointedly looking away to the right. "You?"

"Off on, on off. Mostly off. Not easy being a traveling player."

He nodded, cautiously encouraged. "You got a standing ovation."

"*We* got a standing ov. And no review."

"Four hundred people applauding isn't enough?"

"It's never enough. That's the trouble. I should go to AAA. Approval Addicts Anonymous. Hey..." She found an ice cream wrapper, smoothed it on her knee and wrote her address in Los Angeles and gave it to him. "In case you ever, you know, pass through town."

Cyril nodded deeply and made a show of folding it away in his pocket even though the numbers were already stamped into his mind.

That night he sat in the same row and watched the play again. It was a bigger crowd and there were people seated on either side of him. Last night he'd inhabited the world of a stranger, alone and anonymous and uncertain; now he knew things none of these people did and felt powerful in this new and special status, especially when he overheard remarks about Connie as people read the biographies in the program.

"She's from Vancouver."

"She's the next Nancy Kwan."

"They say she's better. She's got edge."

"*Edge?*"

"It."

"*It?*"

"Positively oozes It."

But his calm confidence began to sour the more he listened. Where was he in all of this? She was passing through, pursuing her career, and he was banging nails and drawing boxes.

The lights went down and the sounds of the Hong Kong bar rose and the curtain opened and there was Suzie Wong dancing with a sailor. Cyril slid deeper into his seat and crossed his arms tightly over his chest. She was leaving tomorrow, less than twenty-four hours. He imagined her life over the following weeks, Toronto, Montreal, New York, hotels, theatres, cabs, cafés, and all too many admirers who had all so much more to offer. At the intermission he left the theatre and walked the same streets he'd walked the night they—the night *she*—had seen *Psycho*.

He was waiting at the exit when Connie appeared and the instant he saw her he knew something was wrong. He approached warily. "What?"

She looked small and haggard and there were tears in her eyes. "What do you mean, *what*?"

"It was too hot," he said, thinking she was insulted that he'd left. "I went for a walk. I missed the second half."

But she wasn't listening, she wasn't even there. "I blanked," she said, staring as if shell shocked. "Just flat out blanked. It's never happened before. Ever."

"Con'. Hey." A couple of cast members including her leading man stood by the theatre entrance.

She didn't respond, she was looking at Cyril, not accusing but wondering, at herself, at him, at the predicament. "I thought of you," she said. "On stage. I thought of you. And then..." She put her fists to her forehead. "The reviewer's gonna kill me. He was there. He interviewed Scotty just now. Oh, God." Her hands dropped to her sides and for a moment Cyril feared she was going to fall to her knees.

"Con'?"

"Be right there," she called, impatience edging her voice. She faced Cyril and took both his hands and he knew it was over.

"It's okay," he said.

"Not really."

"I meant—" But what had he meant?

"I gotta keep my head on straight here."

"I understand."

"It's not just me. There's others. This whole tour."

"Sure. I get it." He nodded vigorously to show he got the idea, that he grasped how important this was, and that he wasn't clinging, that he was not a burden.

"It's just like last time," she said, wondering at some strange déjà vu, and Cyril saw them condemned to travel off through the night on separate paths perhaps to meet up again in another ten years. She touched his face as she had on the occasion of their last farewell, in the IGA, then she began to cry and they embraced and he felt the leather jacket crinkly and sensual, and he held her tightly and kissed her neck and she twisted in his arms and kissed him long and hard on the lips and then she was walking away.

He watched her. "Hey." She stopped and turned. "We're not finished, you know." His tone was not pleading or ominous but a statement, a calm observation of fact.

Her voice was small. "I know."

TWO

THREE DAYS LATER Cyril and Gilbert were on a bus heading for Mexico.

Cyril was unshaved, unwashed, red-eyed, hungover. Gilbert was sporting his Fu Manchu and wore a half dozen candy necklaces of the sort they used to steal from the corner store.

Gilbert had spent much of the past decade driving a taxi, losing on the stock market, losing at the racetrack, losing on pyramid schemes, failing at becoming a private investigator, failing at writing pornography, failing at selling real estate, and failing at marriage. Yet his optimism remained undiminished. As he pointed out to Cyril, his portfolio of life experience was growing ever richer and his potential all but unlimited.

"And now we're heading for Mexico," he said as though it was the crowning achievement.

Mexico, Antarctica, it was all the same to Cyril.

At Bellingham a young marine got on. When he took his

seat he nodded through the window to his parents and then faced forward and looked neither left nor right the entire way to Seattle where, exiting the bus he addressed the driver as sir and when asked said he was flying to Saigon. The driver saluted him and the marine saluted back and the driver said, "Do a job there, son," and the marine said, "I aim to."

Cyril watched the fellow heave his duffel bag onto his shoulder and go out the station door. He imagined his life for the next year, or however long a tour of duty lasted, and wondered if he'd ever return to board a bus back up to Bellingham where his parents would be waiting. He envisioned training camp, the heft of a rifle, the feel of combat boots as he marched into battle and faced enemy fire, smelled cordite and napalm and maybe got hit, and he saw himself wrapped in bandages in a hospital in the jungle breathing the pinched smell of disinfectant.

They stayed three nights in San Francisco and wandered the streets looking for free love and free drugs. The closest they came to free love was a come-on from a store detective with a five o'clock shadow and eye make-up in a Safeway; the closest they came to free drugs was the pot-thick air around the North Beach campfires. At San Diego they walked across the border into Tijuana where Gilbert got his picture taken holding an iguana. Their room at the Pensione Mondragon cost fifty cents and all night long dogs fought in the street. In the morning Cyril and Gilbert ate tortillas the texture of linoleum, red eggs, and peppered potatoes, all washed down with Fanta. Then they proceeded to explore the market with its bewildering variety of chili peppers and edible cacti, and various ornate madonnas, Cyril resolving that on the way back he'd buy a Virgin of Guadalupe for his mother, one encrusted in seashells and Christmas lights. By midday the streets smelled of pee and exhaust, and the very shadows seemed to cringe from the sun.

Along with churches and shops there were cantinas, and inevitably Gilbert led the way through a set of swinging doors to a table set with a shaker of cayenne and a plate of quartered oranges. Mescal and beer arrived. The drill was basic: shake cayenne onto orange, bang back mescal, bite orange, gulp beer. On their third round Cyril began to feel like a beached raft being refloated on an incoming tide. For the first time in days he was able to forget his misery and look around, and what he discovered was that no one in the cantina had any shoelaces, or rather that one man had them all. He was a fat man at his own table in the middle of the room, with a heap of laces before him, and he was now regarding the newcomers with interest. With a downward wave of his fingers he indicated that Cyril and Gilbert were to join him.

"Give to me your shoelace," he said to Cyril.

"Why?"

"Give to me your shoelace."

Cyril looked to Gilbert who, for once, had no advice. Anxious not to offend in a foreign country, Cyril took the lace from one of his Converse All Stars.

"You are strong?" enquired the Mexican.

"No stronger than anyone else, I guess."

The fat man had heavy-lidded eyes and a smooth face and a long black moustache and black hair that hung straight down. "You can break your shoelace I give to you two dollar. I can break your shoelace you give to me two dollar. Is a new shoelace, yes?"

Cyril had got them recently. He nodded.

"Bueno. Try."

It occurred to Cyril that either way he ended up with a broken shoelace, nonetheless he wound the end of the lace around each hand, took a breath and yanked. The lace held. The Mexican laughed the long low laugh of a man who knew his territory. He had beautiful white teeth, not one of them gold.

"Con permiso." He took the shoelace, looped an end around each forefinger, held the lace up for Cyril and Gilbert to see, then popped it. He did this simply, easily, with a mere toss of his wrists. "Two dollar."

Cyril paid and they rose to leave taking the broken halves of his lace, but the man said that it was now Gilbert's turn. When Gilbert had tried, failed, and paid, it was Cyril's turn to try again. "No, no, you win."

The man was sad. "But you are in Rome. You must do as the Romans do. It is the rule. Do you not go by the rule? Everyone here has gone by the rule. You are too good for the rule?" Cyril looked around at the other drinkers who were watching with shy interest, their laceless shoes loose on their feet. The fat man wore white pants, a white shirt, and a red sash for a belt. And he was, Cyril noted, wearing sandals that required no laces.

When they departed, eight dollars poorer, shuffling their feet so as not to lose their shoes, it was evening and shadows filled the streets.

Five days later they reached Mexico City. The cars were foul but the people were gracious and the architecture grand. Cyril's mother had urged him to go to the *Basilica de Nuestra Senora de Guadalupe*, on the hill where a Mexican Indian convert had seen a vision of the Virgin Mary. He and Gilbert dutifully took one of the vw Beetle taxis. The driver was unimpressed by Gilbert's attempt to bond over the fact that they were both cab drivers, perhaps suspecting Gilbert of trying to get a reduced fare.

Cyril sat in a pew and watched worshippers approach the altar on their knees and thought of his childhood catechism classes where he learned of saints and martyrs who put stones in their shoes or crawled over gravel so as to share the agony of Christ. He remembered Father Krasniuk saying each of them had their own guardian angel. "He's there to protect you," he assured them. "You can't see him, but he's there." Father K was young and brisk and smiled a lot and Cyril had liked him. A picture book in catechism class showed a man in a cauldron of boiling oil. There he stood, relaxed, leaning one elbow on the cauldron's edge, chatting with an astonished Roman centurion. Another showed Daniel in the lions' den, the lions as meek as kittens. "That's faith," said Father K, "that's God. He protects His children, and we're all His children." He smiled broadly as he related this Truth. "Have faith. He's looking out for us."

But even at the age of nine Cyril had been doubtful, for if God and the guardian angels were looking out for us then why had they let Stalin come to power? Why had God and His helpers permitted the Holodomor during which millions of Ukrainians starved to death? He was about to ask about this when Frank Stepanik barfed, diverting everyone's attention. Cyril went home and asked his mother but her answer was to grow teary and embrace him so tightly that Cyril very nearly suffocated, as if she was trying to squeeze the very question out of him for he was better off without it.

After the *Basilica de Nuestra Senora de Guadalupe* they went to Trotsky's house and saw the desk where he was ice picked in the back of the head. Trotsky had come to Mexico to escape Stalin, but as Cyril's mother had said—and said again—no one escaped Stalin. He recalled how, back in 1963, when the Free World was mourning the assassination of JFK, his mother wore the grim smile of the vindicated. The Russians may have withdrawn their missiles yet they'd countered with Lee Harvey Oswald, and only the naive could have expected anything less. And clearly the Americans were naive, out maneuvered by the serpent Stalin operating from beyond the grave via Kruschev who, she had no doubt, was in communion with the arch Soviet Satan by seance and every other Rasputin-like medium who had slithered up from the Moscow sewers.

They were staying in a hotel whose floors were slanted due to earthquake damage and whose ceiling fan squeaked like tormented mice. The one window was tall and narrow with slatted wooden shutters. It offered a view of construction cranes as well as battered billboards left over from the Olympic Games four years earlier. Cyril had brought a sketchbook but so far had been too depressed to open it. What he did was walk. He walked the streets from church to church and gallery to gallery, sometimes with and sometimes without Gilbert, trying not to brood over Connie, which was as impossible as turning his back to his own mind, though at least the sights, sounds, and smells of the strange city kept him half a step ahead of it as it taunted him like a spurned beggar.

One afternoon he wandered into an exhibition of Goya etchings and studied the peasants and witches and soldiers, moved by the squat and awkward figures. In a second-hand bookshop with a gritty stone floor and dark wood walls he found an old edition of Da Vinci's drawings. Though the book was discoloured and musty with decay, Cyril bought it and took it back to the hotel room where he stared at the master's drawings as if at a math problem. Such majestic confidence in the lines, each one a gesture of absolute command. Had he worked quickly or with patience? Had he hunched close to the paper or stood back? Had his hand done the work or his head? He stared as if to imprint individual lines into his mind so that he might reproduce them like lines of verse. Experimenting, Cyril found he could draw dynamic lines like whiplashes, stinging with energy, yet how to control them? When he went for control he lost verve and the lines were timid.

Next to the hotel was a desiccated park and across from it a shop that sold Bibles, Virgins, and crucifixes plus it had a life-sized Christ made of clear glass standing in the window. Next to this shop was a bakery. One morning Cyril went in and bought a box of *pan dulces* then sat in the park feeding them to the birds whose flit and murmur diverted him from thoughts of Connie. Two nuns stopped before the window of the religious shop and admired the glass Christ. They leaned close, stepped back, put their heads together and nodded in agreement as if to say yes this was the Saviour for them. Cyril had a pencil but had left his sketchbook so drew the nuns on the lid of the *pan dulce* box. He found himself coordinating each line with either an exhalation or an inhalation, and was cautiously pleased with the results. Usually he held his breath when he drew.

Gilbert joined him, a bottle of Fanta in one hand and a Styrofoam container of tripe and salsa in the other. He held it tantalizingly under Cyril's nose.

"No."

Leaning to admire the sketch of the nuns, Gilbert nodded his approval and then told Cyril, not for the first time, that he should go into forgery.

"You think so?'

"You're never going to make any money selling nuns. Unless they're fucking. Let me show you something."

Cyril accompanied him down the cobbled street to a shop that sold birds. There were parrots, minahs, and macaws. "They'd cost a fortune back in Vancouver."

Cyril did not debate this because for one thing he assumed it was obvious and for another he didn't really care; he was more interested in the way the wire converged in such perfect lines at the tops of the cages.

"I could ship them home and sell them," said Gilbert.

Cyril did not debate that either, because he was busy admiring the lines of the feathers, arranged in perfectly tapering patterns, thinking that if you were looking for proof of a divine Being—a Being with an artistic eye—you'd do better to consider those feathers than stories of guardian angels.

"Birds," said Gilbert, nodding slowly, nodding knowingly, as if it had been clear all along.

Lines, thought Cyril.

They bussed down to the coast and found a fishing village by a river where flamingos strutted and flocks of small green parrots burst from the jungle on one bank and disappeared into the jungle on the other bank. During the afternoon heat everything went quiet; even the sunlight on the water settled into a molten slumber. By evening the mosquitos swarmed and the bats tumbled, and at night the jungle woke with whoops and shrieks and the ringing of cicadas; by dawn they were replaced by the yelps and trills of warblers and gulls along with the dry-throated squawk of grackles. All morning, pelicans glided silently along the line of the breaking surf.

They rented a house with a corrugated metal roof, mud walls, and a packed sand floor. A bare bulb dangled from a wire, there was a hotplate, and when they were thirsty they drank boiled river water cooled in a stone cistern with a wooden lid. Nearby stood a thatch outhouse twitchy with rats.

One evening as they swayed in their hammocks Cyril asked, "Can we change?" He'd voiced the question as much to the night as to Gilbert and expected no answer from either.

"No, but we can become more deeply ourselves."

Gilbert's response had come so quickly, with such assurance, that Cyril set his bare feet on the ground on either side of the hammock and sat up to look at him. It was too dark but he could hear Gilbert's hammock rope strain against the post like ship's rigging.

"What?" asked Gilbert, sensing Cyril's gaze.

"Is that a quote?"

"What's-her-nuts used to say it."

Cyril lay back in the dark and contemplated Gilbert's grandmother buried with that pistol. "Was she deeply herself?"

For a long time Gilbert said nothing and Cyril assumed he'd fallen asleep until his voice came out of the black. "After grandpa offed himself she was."

"How do you know?"

"She said so."

Cyril tried to imagine such a conversation with his own mother. "Did she ever say why he did it?"

"Battle fatigue. Shell shock."

"But it was so long ago."

"What the fuck, Cyril I don't know. Anyway, why do you want to change?" He yawned and scratched his chest luxuriously with both hands.

"Don't you want to make money?" asked Cyril.

"I don't have to change to do that."

"You're broke."

"Wheels are turning," he said contentedly.

Cyril wondered if Gilbert was profound or an idiot. Where did such easy confidence come from? Was it like hair colour or height, something you were simply born with? There seemed no logic to who had it and who didn't.

Gilbert took a boat trip up the river—financed by Cyril—and returned with a parrot in a cage made of saplings. The bird's eyes were red and wrinkled as if it had been weeping. Soon there were two more parrots, then a toucan with a beak as long and sharp as shears, and Gilbert had to hire a carpenter—with money borrowed from Cyril—to build a bigger cage.

"It's cruel," said Cyril.

"It's commerce," said Gilbert, as if Cyril was committing the all too common error of confusing categories and getting moral where morality had no business.

Cyril drew the birds. He also drew the fishing boats, the row boats, the wharf, the canoes and the palm trees and the crab shells and the huts and the sleeping dogs and the church as well as the red '53 Buick of Don Antonio Martin Smolenski, whose grandfather came from Krakow. He drew Don Antonio's antique Spanish rifle with the trumpet-shaped barrel, and drew the dusty iguanas that sat as still as baked clay. He sharpened his pencils with a knife and soon he was working with nothing but a nub on butcher paper. They bussed up the coast to Puerta Vallarta where Gilbert looked into shipping rates for sending the birds north and Cyril bought paper, pencils, and a box of charcoal sticks from a charcoal burner who lived amid sacks of briquets and whose face and knuckles were seamed with soot. They spent the night in a hotel five blocks from the beach and in the morning, before catching their bus, strolled through the town feeling superior to the tourists.

Five months they stayed in San Vicente del Mar, Gilbert acquiring more birds and Cyril drawing more than he had in years. He experimented at using no lines at all, only shades of grey. He went through his own cubist phase, rendering everything in blocks and cylinders. For a while he gave up on representation altogether, devoting all his attention to the character of the line, wide and bold, light and tenuous, thin and sinister, tightly coiled, gently looping.

The local kids came every day to see the birds and to watch Cyril work. Sometimes he drew them and off they'd go, holding their portrait in both hands as if reading a scroll. Don Antonio Martin Smolenski commissioned a portrait, and Cyril devoted two weeks to improving the proud old man's looks by straightening his nose and ignoring the smallpox scars that dented his complexion. He earned twenty us dollars, a slab of tuna, and a bottle of locally distilled mescal plugged with a twist of rag. His first sale.

Don Antonio held Cyril by the shoulders. "To have talent like yours," he said wistfully. The richest man in the village, Don Antonio's bookshelf held works by Albert Camus, José Marti, and Cervantes. He was sixty and had pale blue eyes in a sun-leathered face, and while he'd been to Mexico City and to Vera Cruz he preferred San Vicente.

The village enchanted Cyril. He liked the river's cool scent, the jungle's sweet rot, the booming surf, liked sleeping in the afternoon and waking to the spectacle of sunset, but best of all he loved the dawn when the air was almost chill, the sky cinematic, and the world was cleansed not so much of its sins as the muddled chaos of the previous day.

Once a week he shaved in a mirror the size of a playing card propped on two nails driven into a post. If he stepped back his entire face fit in the mirror; up close only his nose, eye, or mouth. It was this fragmented self-scrutiny that started him on a series of self-portraits. He went to Don Antonio Martin Smolenski's general store to buy a bigger mirror but there wasn't one, so he bought two more small ones and arranged them on a shelf. From a distance he saw three Cyril's; up close he saw himself in pieces.

Then there was the moth, tan and grey, the size of a quarter, attracted to the light on the mirrors. Each day the moth lit upon one of Cyril's reflections. He drew the moth over and over, in pen, pencil, line, shade. The moth was an obedient model, its powdery wings suited to charcoal. He named the moth Gustavo, in honour of Carl Gustav Jung, whose book on dreams he'd once tried to read. It seemed to Cyril that the moth was the unconscious while the butterfly, crass, tacky, superficial in its loud beauty, was the conscious.

Yet in spite of all his efforts, the fear lingered that he was nothing more than a draughtsman, that the fat bastard at the interview had been right. No matter that Don Antonio Martin Smolenski praised him and that the villagers called him *el artiste* and there were regular requests for his services, the kids wanting caricatures, the fishermen usually wanting him to draw their boats, and the girls wishing to look like movie stars.

One of Don Antonio's daughters looked better than a movie star. She had two different coloured eyes and a voluptuous figure. Gilbert lusted after her. "I'd like to bite her ass," he said. "If I could unhinge my jaw, like a snake, I'd bite her whole ass." As if to demonstrate, he opened his mouth as wide as he could.

Cyril looked away. He didn't want to see down Gilbert's throat. They were in their hammocks. Chickens worried the dirt while the parrots in their cages worked the kinks from their necks. Cyril informed him that her name was Remedios, and he agreed that biting her ass would be very satisfying. They grew wistful at the thought of Remedios' ass.

"You realize that Don Antonio'll cut your nuts off if you even look at her ass much less bite it."

"Not when he sees how much dinero the birds get me."

"You think that's all it would take?"

"That's all anything takes."

Cyril hoped he was wrong because in his view Remedios was too good for Gilbert.

One afternoon during a downpour, Gilbert mused on the possibility of collecting and selling rain. "Pure rain water. Not from the ground, but the sky...from God! These cat-lickers'll buy anything if it's from God." Gilbert was Scotch Presbyterian and had inherited the view that Roman Catholics were medieval. He stood in the deluge with his arms wide and face upturned as if embracing the rain of wealth. "Then senior Smellyinski'll pony up what's her name."

"Remedios," said Cyril, irritated. "You're going to hell."

"Maybe. But I'll get there in a Mercedes."

Remedios and two of her sisters came to gaze at Gilbert's birds. While Gilbert deployed the full arsenal of his charm, Cyril watched from the hammock, his drawing pad in his lap. The ladies looked queenly and statuesque even though none stood taller than five foot two. They turned as one to Gilbert with the serene if giddy hauteur of adolescent royalty. Even from thirty yards away Cyril could read the dance-like rite of male-female interaction that was unfolding.

"You like my parrots?"

They smiled.

Cyril judged that all three were in their late teens. He wasn't sure, but the eldest might be married, for he'd seen her with a baby. He dreaded the thought of Gilbert scoring with Remedios. It would make him unbearable, cock-walking around, that maddening self-confidence bolstered yet again. Cyril tried ignoring it all by focusing on his drawing, a man in a straw hat with two long strings of garlic bulbs slung over his shoulders. His face was in shadow, his straw hat frayed, his hands long and sinewy. Hunched over his work detailing the fibres of the hat, Cyril couldn't ignore the three shadows that suddenly darkened the pale sandy dirt. He looked up. The girls stood at a respectful distance, intrigued by what he was drawing but too polite to intrude. He held it up. They murmured.

Remedios nodded and said that the garlic seller's name was Angel. *Ang hell.*

Cyril wrote the name at the bottom of the page.

Gilbert approached, grinning, proprietorial, as if to gather up his harem.

"You can draw me?" Remedios asked.

Cyril could see the pride and yet hesitation in her manner. Her long black hair framed her face as if she was peeking through dark curtains. She was risking rejection. But why would he draw Angel the garlic seller and not her? "Okay."

"Bueno."

The women turned to leave.

"When?" asked Cyril.

"Tomorrow."

"Here?"

She waved her forefinger side-to-side and clucked her tongue once. "No. My house."

Cyril and Gilbert watched the girls depart. Gilbert wasn't angry or jealous at Remedios' interest in Cyril. He was so genuinely surprised it was as if they'd witnessed a quirk of culture, on par with the Chinese regarding live monkey brains as a delicacy.

Cyril showed up at Don Antonio's the next morning at ten, shaved, showered, in a shirt still damp from having washed it at dawn. Don Antonio Smolenski's house was simultaneously elegant and haphazard. Some walls were wood, some breeze block, others palm thatch. Parts of the roof were baked ceramic tiles and others corrugated aluminum sheeting. The fence was cement with broken glass on top, though there were gaps big enough to step through. Dogs howled heralding Cyril's approach.

Remedios met him at the gate, which had a leather strap for a hinge and was flanked by two cement dolphins heavily pitted by the wind-blown sand. Just inside the gate were two enormous nopal cacti on which were snagged scraps of paper, shreds of cloth, and hen feathers. Two carved wooden chairs waited in the dirt courtyard where chickens pecked and laundry dripped. Remedios was wearing a lemon yellow dress that tucked tightly under her bosom and fell to just below her knees. The collar, cuffs, and hem were black ruffles and the buttons on the bodice were copper coins.

"Que linda," he said.

She nodded and then sat in one of the chairs, crossing her legs and presenting him a three-quarter view.

"Don't make her too beautiful," said Don Antonio, joining them. He was barefoot and bare-chested and smoking a cigar. "It will go to her head."

"Papa," she scolded.

The older man directed a look at Cyril that was an appeal for sympathy as well as a warning to him to behave himself, then he turned and departed, smoking his cigar.

Cyril got busy with his pad and pencils and then positioned the other chair. Then he stepped closer, studying her. It seemed strange that she kept so much of her face hidden within the curtains of her hair. He reached out—she flinched. He hesitated, looked at her, and slowly, with his forefinger, folded her hair back behind her ear: and that's when he discovered her scar. It ran like a thin, pale, upturned sickle from the corner of her right eye to the edge of her right nostril. It wasn't huge or even unsightly, rather it was dramatic and intriguing.

She turned to the left, giving him a full view. In a hard voice she asked, "Do you like my mark?"

"Muy bonita. How did you get it?"

"A duel. With my sister Magdalena. We were twelve. She insulted me."

"You insulted me," came a voice.

Magdalena's face appeared in the window of a blue cement wall nearby. Some rapid Spanish was exchanged, then Magdalena went away.

"She is a bitch."

"You are a bitch," came the retort, this time from another window.

"She is my best friend in the world," called Remedios.

"You are my life!" cried Magdalena.

"You have family?" Remedios asked Cyril.

He described his family and she regarded him with what might have been a smile.

She called him Señor Picasso. "Mi ojas aqui," she said, indicating her eyes in their proper places, "no ahi," she added, indicating the side of her head.

"Su ojas muy bonita," he said.

"Y usted muy guapo."

"Gracias."

"Are you famous?" she asked.

He barked a laugh. "No."

She frowned. "Why not?"

He was about to say he was young, but he was ten years older than her.

"Are you rich?"

"Do I look rich?"

"Are you a hippie?"

"No."

"Of course not," she said with deep satisfaction, "hippies are godless drug addicts. You are an artist."

On the day Cyril showed the finished portrait the entire family gathered. He'd managed to find a sheet of window glass, have it cut to size, framed it with thin strips of split bamboo on a panel, and presented himself at noon Sunday in a white shirt that he had not only washed but pressed by laying his Da Vinci book on it and weighing it down with bricks.

Don Antonio Smolenski, his wife Josefina, married daughter Conchita and her husband Fidel and their two daughters, plus Magdalena, Palma, Esmerelda, Gustavina, and Remedios were all present. The unveiling took place in the yard with the hens and dogs and a table laid with a white cloth and a buffet of goat and fish and chicken served in platters and bowls and pots all of baked red clay. No such ceremony had accompanied the drawing of don Antonio himself. At one point Remedios appeared at Cyril's side and hip-checked him lightly and whispered, "Tranquilo."

Still, when he slid the pillowslip from the portrait everyone, including Remedios, was silent. During this silence Cyril's heart thumped so ominously that he wondered what his chances were if he had a stroke here in such a small town. His gaze moved from person to person starting with Don Antonio and ending with Remedios. She was expressionless. Then, as though returning from an out-of-body experience, her lidded eyes blinked and the corners of her mouth curled upward in a smile and she nodded. "Muy bueno. Mucho gusto." Don Antonio shook his hand then poured drinks.

During the ten days Cyril had worked on the portrait, Gilbert had continued amassing birds. He now had twelve parrots, a few large and wrinkled, most small and green, three toucans, three macaws, and half a dozen brilliantly coloured creatures whose names he couldn't get straight. The rainy season was approaching, and the next step was to arrange the transport and deal with the paperwork, tasks involving tortured discussions with various officials of vague authority. Cyril, whose Spanish was better, accompanied him.

"You must pay the *mordida*," one sympathetic *jefe* informed the gringos with a deep sadness at such a state of affairs as he held out his hand for money.

Gilbert rated himself too worldly to be shocked, and informed Cyril that was the price of doing business when he borrowed yet more money from him. So absorbed was Gilbert in the complexities of his project that he had forgotten about biting Remedios' ass and was indifferent to how close Cyril was getting. Remedios had taken to passing by their hut two and three times a day on her way to and from the market, nodding and occasionally deigning to converse.

Don Antonio sent a message inviting Cyril for a talk. Smolenski's study was not an example of baronial splendour, but it did aspire. The floor was made of broad planks of oiled mahogany, there were blue and white ceramic candlesticks in the shape of nymphs, there were sea shells the size of footballs, a rack of pool cues though no pool table, an old clock, black and white photographs dating to 1880s Krakow, one showing a boy on the shoulders of a man in front of a small stone church. Smolenski indicated that Cyril should sit in the chair matching his own. They were carved wood and cracked leather, with ball and claw feet and high backs. Between them was a three-legged table on which sat a decanter of smoky liquor and two small glasses with gold trim. Smolenski poured, raised his glass, "Nostrovia amigo," drank it in one go then set the glass down with a rap. Cyril dutifully followed. He managed not to gag even though it felt he'd gulped a burning coal directly from a forge. Smolenski gazed out the glassless window. The sea glittered in the late afternoon sun. His eyes were half shut as though he was either falling asleep or meditating on some deep subject. Eventually the old man directed his formidable attention upon Cyril. "You love her?"

Cyril stared at the seamed and striated face so bluntly confronting him. The nostrils were long and dark and the whites of the blue eyes as yellowed as old piano keys. Cyril found himself nodding.

"She loves you."

Again Cyril nodded.

Smolenski refilled their glasses and again they drank. He pointed to the oldest photograph, "My great great-grandfather as a child."

Cyril nodded a third time. He tried imagining the journey of that boy from Poland to Mexico and the many crises and adventures that must have occurred en route. What had made him leave? What had made him choose Mexico? Or had it all been an accident, a stumble from one side of the world to the other? Cyril looked at the decanter on the table. "What is this stuff?"

"Mezcal."

It tasted like motor fuel.

"There won't be much dowry," warned Smolenski. "There are four sisters."

Cyril swallowed.

"A small house. A small piece of land. Goats. A boat. It leaks but you can fix it. You can work with wood?"

"Yes."

"Good. And you can do your other work. Your real work."

Cyril saw what was being presented: a life with a beautiful woman in a beautiful place where he could pursue his work. He settled into his chair and shut his eyes feeling a deep relief. He thought of Gilbert and his birds, of his mother and the cemetery, and of Paul and his numbers, and all the while the mezcal warmed his blood and his heart beat to the tick of the old clock and his gratitude was immense. I'm here, he thought, I've arrived. When he opened his eyes he turned to Don Antonio Martin Smolenski and with great solemnity put his right hand over his heart and said, "You do me a great honour, but I cannot marry Remedios."

Smolenski frowned.

Cyril stood.

"Is it her scar?"

"No. She's beautiful. I'm sorry. I have to go."

He didn't go straight back to their hut but walked off along the beach, hands deep in his pockets and shoulders hunched. The sun was setting and birds shrilling in the jungle. The waves washed up the shore and then hissed back down leaving the sand seething. His mind was blank, stunned, as though deafened by an explosion. A wind gusted up and while it kept the evening rush of mosquitoes at bay it spat sand in his face. He didn't care, he kept walking.

Long before he returned he heard Gilbert's shouting and saw parrots swirling into the red sky and burning pages tumbling past. There was Gilbert chasing back and forth. He lunged and missed and fell to his knees and stayed there, exhausted, defeated. Cyril didn't even take his hands from his pockets. He watched his scorched drawings scud away into the night. Resting a consoling hand on Gilbert's back he tried to think of something to say but no words came.

Gilbert had plenty to say the next morning on the bus north.

"It's your fault."

"I'm sorry."

"You could have bit her ass."

Cyril nodded.

"What's his nuts liked you," said Gilbert, a bewildered emphasis on the word *liked*.

"Yup."

"Fucking up your stuff, okay, I get it, you insulted him, but why screw me around?"

Cyril felt bad.

Gilbert leaned his head in his hands.

Gazing out the window at the green wall of gnarled and impenetrable jungle sliding past, Cyril wondered what lived in there? Snakes, bugs, lizards? Maybe some of Gilbert's birds?

∽   ∾

They flew from Puerta Vallarta to Los Angeles. Cyril had enough money left for one bus ticket to Vancouver. He gave it to Gilbert.

Calmer now, Gilbert said no, they could hitchhike.

Cyril insisted. "Go. Please. I owe it to you. Besides, I need some time."

Gilbert studied him. "You're an idiot."

"I'd say we've pretty much established that fact."

"Does she know you're coming?"

Cyril shook his head.

"My idea was sound," said Gilbert, meaning his birds.

"It was."

"There's real money there."

"You can try again," said Cyril.

They shook hands.

∽ ∾

Wrought iron letters were bolted to a troweled arch that opened onto a quadrangle of parked cars, withered shrubs, and long-stay motel rooms. At each corner ravaged palm trees looked as though they'd been used for target practise. Some sort of flying beetle motored past his face and struck a lamp pole, reeled and then continued on. He assembled the facts: at the age of seventeen Connie had known what she wanted and had gone after it; she'd dumped him twice and now here he was about to knock on her door, an act of admirable tenacity or foolish thick-headedness. But he reminded himself that he was merely passing through town and popping in to say hello, which was the truth, sort of. He turned around. A panhandler sat cross-legged on the sidewalk; Cyril turned and faced the motel. He'd phoned but there'd been no answer, he'd written from San Vicente but never heard back. A hint? A sign? Or merely the Mexican postal system?

Scanning the second floor he spotted room 209 at the far end. His mouth was dry and his pulse pounded. Los Angeles was gritty and arid in contrast to the syrupy humidity of San

Vicente. There was the racket of radios and car horns instead of the cries of gulls and throbbing of cicadas. He'd bought her a bracelet of Taxco silver, no big deal, a token, and he touched his shirt pocket reassuring himself it was still there and then reminding himself that she probably wasn't home anyway—who was home on a Wednesday afternoon? He'd slip the bracelet under the door with a note, or maybe without a note, just let it lie there mysterious and intriguing, and when they next met, for they would meet, of that he had no doubt, he could ask her casually about her silver bracelet and tell her the story of how he took a trip from the Mexican coast up into the mountains to Taxco with its steep streets and silversmiths and bought it for her.

꩜   ꩜

Leaving Connie's, Cyril dropped the bracelet into the panhandler's hat. At the end of the street two guys stepped from some bushes wielding sharpened pencils.

"Fuckin' pay up, cocksucker."

Cyril raised his hands palms outward. "I haven't got anything."

"Fuck you, pay up." The mugger was lean and sunburned and grubby and his nose was running. He wiped his forearm across his upper lip then thrust the sharpened pencil upward like a knife fighter. Cyril stepped back. The other guy was big though swaying as if drunk. He made an overhand stab. Cyril raised his arm and fended off the blow and the guy stumbled past on his own momentum. The other thrust again but the pencil slid between Cyril's ribs and elbow and Cyril found himself nose-to-nose with him, his arm clamped under his own. The guy smelled of pee and sweat. A moment passed during which neither knew what to do. Then Cyril hoisted upward on the guy's arm hyper-extending his elbow. The guy howled and stood on his toes. They stayed this way, as if in some strange dance. The one yipping while his partner got up and advanced.

Cyril hoisted higher. "I'll break his arm."

The little one shrieked and the other halted.

"Get going," said Cyril, and held on until the big guy was down the street by the panhandler who was just sitting there watching. The big mugger halted and said something to him—then grabbed the guy's hat and ran. Cyril released the little guy, who dropped to his knees cradling his arm.

"I should have stayed in San Vicente," said Cyril.

"What? Are you fucking nuts?"

"I must be," he admitted.

He'd looked through a gap in the slats of Connie's venetian blinds and seen that they were shooting a film—there was a cameraman and a sound man—and there was Connie in bed with two men, one black, one white.

THREE

CYRIL ACCOMPANIED GILBERT to the cab depot where he met Lemuel, the dispatcher, who was eating the third of five hotdogs that were laid in a row on his desk. On Gilbert's advice, Cyril had brought along a bottle of Ballantyne's. He gave Lemuel the whisky, Lemuel gave him a set of keys, and Gilbert led him to a car.

"I got something for you," said Gilbert conspiratorially. Reaching into the black leather briefcase in which he carried his racing forms, his *Wall Street Journal*, and his Hoagie, he shoved a .38 into Cyril's hand. "Keep it here." He indicated a spot under the left side of the driver's seat. When Cyril pointed out that he was right-handed, Gilbert said to start practising with his left.

"Why would I want a job like this?"

Gilbert counted on his fingers. "Be your own boss. Meet interesting people. Have time to read, draw, cogitate, harass women, whatever you want. Anyway, I've never had to use mine," he said. "Consider it a guardian angel."

Guardian angels hadn't proven too effective as far as Cyril could see, so he didn't put much faith in the gun. Nonetheless, he had to admit that driving was diverting, and even if he wasn't really his own boss but more like a dog on a long leash, he enjoyed the pleasing delusion of independence, and it made a welcome change from construction. Most of the trips were short and many people were content to ride in silence which was fine with him. He thought often of Connie and felt naive at his shock at what he'd seen. He imagined the financial desperation that had driven her to it. Had her acting career tanked? The theatre tour bombed? Maybe that was why she'd never responded to his letter from Mexico. He considered driving the cab all the way down the coast to her motor court, parking right there beneath her door and honking the horn and when she stepped out asking if she'd called a cab, charming her with the sheer unabashed whimsy of the stunt.

His first week driving went well enough: people were polite, they tipped, they got out. By the end of the week he was taking his sketchbook with him and when things got slow he did a little work, street scenes, pedestrians, lampposts. Then he switched to evenings where, according to Gilbert, the good money lived. At first Lemuel fed him easy trips. He drove some suits, some office girls, ferried some Korean sailors to the Seaman's Club. Then there was a lull. Along with his sketchpad he had a textbook on Ukrainian History because he was considering going back to school. Paul once said Ukrainian Cossacks invaded Siberia in the late sixteenth century by carrying their riverboats over the Urals. Why anyone would want to invade Siberia mystified Cyril, but it was an impressive feat that sparked his curiosity. He was flipping through a chapter titled *The Glory That Was Kiev* when the cab doors swung open and two guys dropped into the back and a third hit the front causing the car to lurch on its springs.

"My man! A hearty good evening. What're you reading there?"

Cyril showed him the cover.

The kid plucked it from his hand. "Rooshyuh," he said in a movie accent.

"Where to?"

"Know any fuck-houses?" demanded one in the back.

"Yeah, we want to get us some." As if choreographed, the two in back raised their fists and pumped their hips rocking the car.

Cyril took his book from the kid's hand and said he didn't know any brothels. The guys were in their twenties, drunk, wearing sports shirts and jeans, clean-shaven, with good haircuts; suburban boys on the slum.

The two in the back reached for the doors to get out, but the one up front was apparently intrigued by Cyril and, settling himself deeper in the seat, directed Cyril to just drive.

"Just drive where?"

He pointed in the direction the car was facing. "Just drive that way."

Gilbert had warned him about this. He'd also warned him to keep his doors locked to prevent anyone getting in before he'd had a chance to give them the once over. "I need a destination."

"Need or want?" asked the kid. He was big, with a meaty head and thick hair and heavy dark eyes. His T-shirt was expensive, Cyril could tell by the cut of the collar, not your three-for-one deal from Fields. "It's important to distinguish need from want," he advised.

"Okay, I need *and* want a destination."

"Methinks you're avoiding the issue."

"No, the issue is you should find another car," said Cyril.

The kid became sad. He exhaled long and he pouted. "You don't like us."

Cyril's glance flicked to the rearview. The two in back had tensed, like dogs at the alert, and he feared one would grab him around the neck. It was about eight o'clock and dark, a misty rain obscuring the windshield and blurring the lights of the shops that seemed far away down the suddenly empty stretch of Hastings. "You'll have better luck with another cab," he repeated in a more reasonable tone, as if genuinely eager to see their wants and needs satisfied.

"You don't like us and I don't think you trust us."

Cyril rested his left hand on his left thigh and took a slow breath and thought of the .38 just inches from his hand. "I'm trying to work."

"And we want to offer you our custom. But you refuse to take us to a house where we can get our ills reputed." He leaned to read Cyril's driver ID. "Cyril Andrachuk."

The two in back chuckled.

The one next to him rediscovered the text book on the seat between them. He picked it up with exaggerated care and slowly fanned the pages and came to a marker. "Ah. Stalin. You're reading about the man who fucked your people up the ass without even the courtesy of lubricant." He raised the book high for the benefit of his pals, as though it was a Bible and he was a preacher. "Stalin killed more people than Hitler. Did you know that? Stalin is the nightmare from which Russia has yet to awake. A man of charisma and cunning. A beast worshipped as a god. How I'd love to have met him. Purely in the interest of psychology, you understand." He returned the book to the seat and gave it a fond pat. Then he mused, "I wonder if fucking a country is better than fucking a cunt?" The boys in back hee-hawed. "What do you think, Cyril?"

"I think it's time for you to get out." Gripping the .38 he swivelled so that his back was braced against the door and pointed the gun at the kid's head.

When they were on the sidewalk, Cyril started the car and drove to the depot and gave Lemuel the keys, his trip sheet, announced that he was quitting, and went to his mother's, where he'd been living since his return from Mexico while he looked for a place of his own. The next day two cops showed up and informed him that charges had been laid. It went before a judge who, while not unsympathetic to the three-on-one odds, observed that the gun was unregistered and thought that Cyril had overreacted. And while he gave him a suspended sentence it also meant that Cyril now had a criminal record.

∽ ∾

He got on with a house painter named Norbert Hek. On the first day Hek strode into the room Cyril was painting and stood with his hands on his hips and said he was worried. Roller in hand, Cyril asked what exactly Hek was worried about? It was hard to judge Hek's age, he could be forty, he could be sixty, his skin was seamed, he was missing two teeth on the upper left side of his jaw, his eyes were grey and dry and his hair long and blond and brittle. "I'm worried about your relationship with the wall," said Hek. They were undercoating the interior of a newly built house. "About your relationship with the surface." With his fingertips he stroked the drying paint testing for ridges. "You've got to love the surface. I was listening to the sound of your roller. It doesn't sound to me like you care about the surface." Cyril was impressed that Hek could hear the sound of his roller from the next room and furthermore that he could read so much into this sound. As if hearing Cyril's thoughts, he said, "Smack, smack, smack. That's how it sounded."

"Smack, smack, smack?"

Hek nodded. "Slow down. Stroke it." He stroked the air. "Caress it. Make it feel good." He ran his fingers—thick, stubby, paint scabbed—over the paint as though reading poetry in Braille. "Feather it out."

"Okay."

"Make it smooth."

Cyril nodded.

"Think of skin."

"Skin."

"A woman's thigh," said Hek. "Right here." He ran his palm down the inside of his leg, from groin to knee. He was wearing baggy white pants stained with various pale shades of paint. "Okay?"

"Okay." Cyril nodded to reassure him that he grasped the concept. Hek was about to go back to his own work when he said, "People don't touch enough. We're all eye. The eye should lead to the flesh. Me, I see a well-painted wall I want to get naked and press up against it." He pressed himself to the

Gyproc. Maintaining this position, he turned his head so that he could make eye contact and thus drive home his point. "You should want to make love to the wall."

Cyril maintained a politely attentive expression.

"Understand?"

"Got it."

Hek gave three grunting thrusts against the wall with his pelvis then left the room saying, "Now let's see what those other monkeys are up to."

Cyril quit at the end of the day. Yet he had made two discoveries. First, even an idiot like Hek could succeed as a painting contractor; and, second, that he liked painting. The process was soothingly silent in contrast to the whack of hammers and the shriek of saws. A few days later he hooked up with a crew run by a sleepy-eyed German named Irwin who said he'd been, "Painting since I'm thirteen years." There were half a dozen others on the crew. Irwin told them where to paint and they went at it with minimal interruption. If nothing else, painting seemed a step closer to drawing and Cyril felt a natural aptitude, discovering that painting a wall was like painting his mind: you covered one mood with another. Pale grey could be warmed up or a hot yellow could be cooled off. His mind wandered as he painted, though rarely profoundly. My mind mindlessly meanders, he said to himself. My mindlessly meandering mind. My meanderlessly mindering mind... He recalled a *Three Stooges* episode where Curly accidentally swaps Moe's coffee with a can of paint and Moe takes a swallow. "Why you numbskull!" he says, and jabs two fingers in Curly's eyes.

Irwin was a philosopher of paint. He had theories about red and blue and green and yellow and black. "Red is not rage.

Don't let anyone tell you red is rage. It is not rage. I get mad I don't see red I see black. Red is blood, yes, and violence maybe, but violence can be joy, communion, wine, sunset. Blue is the ice of the Virgin Mary's eyes. Green is the wall of a madhouse but is also grass and forest. God is green, green as a frog."

Cyril was not inclined to argue with Irwin about anything, certainly not the colour of God. He nodded his acceptance of the notion that God was green. It certainly seemed as good a colour as any for the Creator. Wondering about the effects of decades of paint fumes on Irwin's brain, Cyril decided to invest in a respirator for whenever he used a spray gun, and at the very least be sure the windows were wide open when he used a brush or roller. Wasn't it lead-based paint that caused Goya to go deaf and mad?

"But you know why people really love paint?" asked Irwin with more than a hint of disgust.

Cyril was eager to hear Irwin's theory. Painters it seemed had a lot of theories. "Why?"

"Because they can cover up the past."

In the evenings Cyril resumed classes with Novak, who was interested to hear about his Mexican adventures and said, quite frankly, that he was surprised Cyril had come back at all. Cyril said he was wondering the same thing. He'd described Don Antonio Martin Smolenski and his daughter Remedios, though made no mention of Connie.

He also enrolled in Ukrainian History. The course had two parts, lecture and tutorial. The professor was a short, thick, middle-aged woman who outlined the course content and expectations in terms of exams and grades, as well as codes of conduct—no swearing, no sexist or racist language, no eating and no drinking. After the fifty-minute lecture they broke into tutorials of another fifty minutes, each led by a graduate student. Cyril found his room. At the front stood a young man of about twenty-five years of age holding a paper cup of coffee which, when Cyril entered, fell from the fellow's hand and splattered on the floor. The guy from the cab. All the other students turned questioningly toward Cyril who merely stood there. The tutorial leader said nothing, just went to the intercom and punched some numbers and within minutes two security guards arrived. The tutorial leader followed Cyril and the guards into the corridor.

"How did you find me?"

"I wasn't looking for you. I'm only here to take the class."

"I can't have violence in my classroom."

"Who's violent?"

"You threatened me with a gun."

"There were three of you," said Cyril, controlling his tone. "You wouldn't get out of my cab. It was you guys who were threatening me."

"We never laid a hand on you."

"You were mad that I wouldn't take you to a whorehouse."

The tutorial leader's gaze wavered. The security guards were following the debate with mounting interest. "I allow that my colleagues and I were somewhat intoxicated."

"The three of you refused to get out of my cab when I politely asked that you do so. All I wanted was to be left alone. I can't believe you brought charges," said Cyril, as if having been betrayed by an old friend. "It was a complete misrepresentation of the facts."

"That's not what the judge thought." He consulted his wristwatch and became fatigued. "Now this has all been very interesting, but I have a responsibility to this institution and to those people in that classroom. And I cannot in good conscience accept as a student a man who threatens people with a gun."

And with that Cyril was escorted to the parking lot and off the campus.

PART THREE – 1982

In Which Cyril Strikes a New Match

ONE

WHEN THE MODEL let her black robe drop to stand naked before the drawing class, Cyril saw a being cast down from Olympus and condemned to live among mortals. She was six-foot-one, had dark red hair to her hips, breasts like ski jumps, and teeth like a horse. As she took her pose, one foot propped on a stool and hands on her hips, she studied each artist in turn. When her gaze reached Cyril it halted. He stopped drawing. She smiled a shrug of a smile as if to say, *Well, here we are, you and I, creatures, beings, alive and above all absurd, but with a destiny to fulfill.* Later, he would insist that he'd read all this and more into that brief smile.

When the session ended she looked over his shoulder then reached for his stick of charcoal and wrote her phone number in the corner. He invited her for a beer at the Europe. Her name was Yvonne, she was Quebecois, had lived a year in the Canaries and two years in India where she'd practised hatha yoga. She wanted to be an actress, but her size was proving problematic.

"I am too high," she said. "Maybe I can be Amazon or robot, but there are not so many calls for Amazon and robot." She looked glum. She picked up her beer glass and ran her tongue along the rim. Then she brightened. "But I am jazz singer, too."

Cyril nodded encouragingly. Modelling, acting, singing. "How about dancing?" He could see her in a chorus line or a ballet.

"Of course," she said as if it was too obvious to mention.

They stayed until closing then he drove her home. She lived in a basement suite off Commercial Drive with a ceiling so low her hair brushed the light fixtures. She made coffee with sweetened condensed milk and Nescafé, and told him how the landlord, Giancarlo, promised to leave her the house if she married him.

He asked, "When's the wedding?"

She let loose a loud piratic laugh.

Cyril said, "If he's old and going to die soon maybe you should."

"Would you?"

"Who knows?"

She regarded him as though he'd revealed a facet she'd not anticipated but of which she approved. "You should find some old woman who will support you."

"Okay."

She was serious. "You must 'ave show. Old ladies will come. They will discover you."

They were seated on a battered couch. Yvonne sprawled at one end, legs crossed at the knee, bare foot bouncing provocatively. She stretched out her arm and clicked the radio on and began to sing along, "You've got the eyeeee of a tiiii-*gerrr*..."

Cyril was drunk. What rogues they were, plotting away in her lair. He grew bold. Leaning toward her he caught her foot in his hands and kissed her ankle and ran his tongue up her calf.

They became lovers. One morning at Cyril's place Yvonne asked if he thought the soul had a colour.

"Sure. Grey."

This troubled her. "But I think it is sapphire or gold."

He said how a house painter he once knew said God was green like a frog. But as for the soul Cyril thought it was grey and had the texture of ashes.

Yvonne was aghast. "Ashes are burnt. The devil is ashes. God is flower or waterfall. The soul is rainbow."

"You think so?"

"But it is obvious!"

"Okay," he said, willing to be proved wrong.

"Slavs are miserable," she said. "In love with their own defeat."

He wondered about that.

Yvonne was a gazelle. She liked to lounge in bed, take naps, lie on the beach, do the backstroke in the ocean with long slow sweeps of her long elegant arms. She'd model for him and then they'd make love pretending they lived in a *rive gauche* garret. Most nights together were spent at his place. He'd found an airy third floor suite with a northwest view in a vast old house that caught the sunset. He liked when Yvonne left clothes and magazines and jewellery. He liked arriving at Novak's class hand-in-hand with her. The Hungarian marked this without comment though Cyril saw approval, or was it amusement, in his eyes.

One evening after class she asked if her posing before other people bothered him.

He said yes.

"But they are all women."

"They look at you."

"They are supposed to look at me."

He shrugged.

"You could 'ave them," she said.

"Who?"

"The women in the class."

"Which one?"

She grimaced as though he was simple. "All of them."

Cyril was intrigued and yet unsettled. Was this an invitation to pursue other women, to have an open relationship? They'd been seeing each other for three months. "I'm not interested."

She smiled as if he'd passed her little test.

Wherever Yvonne went she drew looks. This bothered Cyril. He hadn't introduced her to Gilbert, who was between marriages, and therefore on the prowl. Cyril liked it being just the two of them, it added an element of fantasy, their own private world, separate and far away.

Yvonne knew he went to his mother's most Sunday evenings. "Why you don't show me to your family? You are embarrassed?"

"Come this week."

She turned her head way. "I'm busy."

They were seated by the window in a pair of deep wicker thrones that Cyril had bought at Value Village. It was late October, the sun down, the leaves turning, the grass still pale, the last scent of summer lingering. "Come."

She looked at him, eyes wet. "Okay."

Paul and Della were already there. Yvonne stood a full five inches taller than Della, who was five inches taller than Paul.

"How's the air up there?" he asked.

"I can see for mile," she said. She shook hands with Cyril's mother, praised her Virgin Marys, then joined Della on the couch.

"Where are the boys?" asked Cyril.

"Steve has a car now. They'll be fashionably late."

"I didn't get a car until I was twenty-three," said Paul, proud, bitter, bemused. He looked pale and shaky. Cyril didn't remark on this because it would only incite his brother's rancour.

Yvonne put her hand on Della's knee. "Your boys, they are how old?"

"Seventeen. Twins."

"Do they read each other's mind?"

"They fight," said Paul from the padded chair in the corner. He looked as foul as a chamber pot.

"Brothers," said Yvonne. "I 'ave three and they beat each other black and blue from day one."

Della nodded wearily.

Helen had placed herself on a small wooden chair the better to study the fantastical Yvonne. Cyril knew what she was thinking: was she daughter-in-law material, was she going to give her more grand-children?

Yvonne had braided her hair in a thick red hawser that she draped forward over her shoulder. The normally reticent Della was fingering it as though it was embroidery. Della's hair was combed straight back and she wore white jeans and a tight black top and a strand of red coral. Yvonne wore a black pullover and red jeans, had a large red stud in her nostril and hoop earrings the size of handcuffs.

Cyril bustled about getting drinks, scotch to Paul, red wine to Yvonne, Della, and his mother. For all that she was dour and self-assured, this evening his mother seemed small and frail and uncertain, as if she was drifting out to sea on an iceberg. It was a desolate realization, but he understood that she was old, that she was ignored, that neither her opinion nor presence much mattered, and hadn't since she was no longer required as a babysitter for Chuckie and Steve. If Cyril and Yvonne gave her grand-children she might return to the world of the living.

When Chuckie and Steve arrived, Steve was leading the way as usual. He wore a short, black leather jacket, collar up, hair artfully greased, a few days of equally artful stubble on his chin, a small ring in one ear. He entered through the kitchen twirling the keys of his new car and abusing Chuckie with jovial contempt.

"No one cares, Chucko," he stated with finality. "Karl Marx, Groucho Marx, no one. Not even you. You're just churning air." Having dealt with his brother, Steve went straight to his grandmother and by the time he reached her his swagger had magically transformed into courtliness. He kissed her. She reached to put her palm to his cheek and he hovered just long enough that she might know the glory that was him before turning and acknowledging everyone else. He shook hands with Yvonne who appeared highly entertained by this young blade.

Chuckie was eating two slices of bread plucked from the dinner table. He stopped chewing long enough to kiss his grandmother who made no attempt to stroke his face. He wore a grey sweatshirt and faded jeans. His reddish hair hung uncombed and his stubble, not at all artful like Steve's, was itchy to look at. He was overweight, though moved with a bearlike grace.

"Well?" demanded Paul.

"Friday," said Steve.

Paul nodded severely. He'd bought Steve an old Datsun on the understanding that he'd pay him back in instalments. So far not a dime had arrived.

They moved to the dinner table. Pork, gravy, brussel sprouts, potatoes. Helen Andrachuk remained faithful to her traditional cuisine, her one concession—after years of pleading from Cyril—was to forego cabbage except in the form of coleslaw. Everyone ate heartily except Paul. Della put her palm to his forehead.

He pushed it away. "I'm fine."

"You're pale."

"I'm fine."

"How did you meet?" Helen asked Yvonne.

"Art class. I am model."

"Novak," Helen said sceptically.

"And I sing. I 'ave gig next month at the Classical Joint."

"Congratulations!" said Della.

Helen's mouth worked silently as if translating the real meaning of these words. Model? Singer? Paul went to the couch and stretched out, arm across his brow. Della went to her bag and consulted an array of pill bottles. She gave him some water and tablets and a cool cloth for his forehead. Conversation resumed at a subdued volume. By eight-thirty

Paul and Della had gone home. Steve made some calls and announced he was off to the Ridge to see *Stop Making Sense*.

Chuckie laughed. "Spam for drones."

"What're *you* gonna do? Put on your Mao hat and read his Little Red Book?"

"You're the monkey in the uniform."

Steve shook his head scornfully.

"Behold the rebel, the rogue, the renegade," mocked Chuckie. "Terror of the bourgeoisie."

Steve kissed his grandmother, tossed them all a jaunty wave, and departed jingling his keys. Cyril cleared the table and did the dishes while Chuckie watched the news and Helen made conversation with Yvonne.

ᕦ ᕤ

Cyril accompanied Yvonne to her performance at the Classical Joint. He'd often heard her break into riffs, bits of scat, random shrieked notes, as if she was Ella Fitzgerald trying to shatter a wine glass. Her voice was undeniably powerful.

It was a Friday night. The Classical Joint was in a narrow turn of the century building in Gastown, with brick walls and a high ceiling and mismatched tables and chairs. Cyril had been there with Gilbert, it being one of the few places in the city open after midnight.

Yvonne was relaxed. She entered the Joint as if she owned it. She presented Cyril to Andreus, the urbane Austrian manager with a chinstrap beard. She introduced Cyril to the sax and bass who would be backing her up, two opium-eyed wraiths.

"Man."

"Hey."

They looked from Cyril to Yvonne and back to Cyril, as if wondering how the two of them fit together. Cyril needed a drink. There was no liquor license, but you could order special coffee which arrived with a shot of whisky. Cyril had one, then another, while Yvonne conferred with her musicians. The place soon filled up. People paid their respects, leaning close to Yvonne and whispering in her ear and she throwing her head back and laughing. Cyril had not seen this side of her life. He felt intrigued and abandoned. At about ten in the evening, responding to some secret signal, Yvonne rose and led the sax and bass to the small stage to a spatter of whistles and applause. Then everyone fell silent. Yvonne struck an undeniably impressive figure. Her hair hung long and loose over her bare shoulders, she wore a black tank top that highlighted her magnificent breasts, and an Indian print skirt that swirled about her thighs. She rolled the mic like a fine cigar in her fingers.

The sax opened with low, lamenting notes and then the bass joined in, muted and sad, and then Yvonne began to sing. No one would deny that it was heartfelt. But from her first note—if it was indeed a note—the crowd was uneasy. Within minutes they were exchanging awkward and sceptical glances. Soon some were smirking while others bore expressions of horrified embarrassment. Cyril watched it all. But mostly he watched Yvonne, impressed at how she ploughed ahead, indifferent or oblivious, it was impossible to say which. Maybe she was just too far advanced for them. Maybe she was on another plane. In his heart he knew she stunk. When she finally took a break an hour later most people fled. Yvonne, sweating, exhilarated, rejoined

Cyril at his table. She kissed him, moist and hot and vibrant. He hugged her tightly as if to stop her from going back up on stage, to keep her close and safe from any further humiliation. He pleaded silently for a power failure. Apparently she was only warming up. The second set went on for an hour and forty minutes. When she was finally done Cyril and Andreus were the only ones in the place, even the street people who'd slipped in taking refuge from the rain having vanished.

It was two AM when they got back to Cyril's.

They were still in his van when she turned to him. "What did you think?"

"Great."

She shifted to face him. "You're bullshitting."

"No."

"You think I don't see 'ow everyone bugger off? Fucking Vancouver. Little ass shithole town." She shook her hair back, disgusted.

Cyril was tortured.

"I'm good," she said, defiantly. Then she was sobbing.

Cyril hugged her. "You are. Really. You just need practice. Maybe some voice lessons."

She shoved him away. "You're supposed to be loyal! You're supposed to be behind me!"

"I am."

"'Ow far? Ten mile?"

"Let's go in."

"I don't need lessons. I'm a natural. Anyway, what do you know? You're just some guy who draws."

TWO

CYRIL HAD HATED hospitals ever since he'd worked in one, hated their look, their sounds, and most especially their smell of disinfectant and death. But he dutifully went to visit Paul. A small television was suspended on a mechanical arm above the bed. A program was on about government reparations to the Japanese interned during World War II. There was Mulroney, professionally solemn, absurdly long-jawed, apologizing with that grave voice to the Japanese Canadians for the terrible injustice they had endured.

Paul was smiling his bitter smile. "Funny how they never apologized for interning the Ukrainians in World War One. And how about the Holodomor? Not a word from Gorbachev about that." Paul's smile became even more bitter, his entire face twisting. "Twenty grand each we're giving the Japs. Nice."

"Should be ten times that," said Cyril.

"Maybe," said Paul. "Twenty grand I could go to Mexico and buy a kidney."

"You could go to Ukraine and buy two," said Chuckie.

Seated in one of the green vinyl armchairs across the room, Helen hardened her jaw and continued weeping silently. Chuckie and Steve stood one on either side of their father's bed, while Cyril stood at the foot beside Della.

When they'd first got the news about Paul's condition the doctor had ushered them into his office and invited them to sit and then explained that a kidney transplant was Paul's only hope. Short-haired and tight-collared, the doctor was as grave as a priest. The gift of a kidney was the thing they must hope for, because they were in very short supply.

On the drive home from the hospital Cyril's mother had said, "Give him one of yours." Her tone suggested he had all kinds of kidneys rattling around inside him.

Cyril hadn't said no. But he'd hesitated. And as he did, he felt her watching him, felt her stare burning like a torch into the side of his face. He felt sick and selfish because he didn't want to give up one of his kidneys. "Okay," he said, nodding his head profoundly, as though he hadn't been hesitating at all, that of course he'd do it, he'd only appeared to hesitate because he was concentrating on the road. "Okay," he said again, and for a while they drove in silence. "But maybe we should also consider options. Get another opinion. You know? Just to be sure." He tried to sound relaxed and reasonable.

His mother's response to relaxed and reasonable was to slap him so hard he nearly drove into an oncoming truck.

When he pulled up in front of the house his face was still scorched while his mother's was ice. She'd never forgive or forget. He was selfish and ungrateful and had a soul like smoke. She got out in silence and slammed the door. He leaned across and yelled after her, "I said I'll do it."

The next day Cyril came by to take her to the hospital but

she wasn't home. When he got to Paul's room she was already there, having called a cab. She sat with her chin up and head averted as if he was a stench.

"You look like shit," said Paul.

"You look great," said Cyril.

"I could dance."

Cyril took a deep breath and announced, "I'll give you one of mine."

It was as though curtains had been flung wide and a window opened admitting fresh air. Steve and Chuckie stepped forward and shook Cyril's hand and gripped his shoulder. Was the relief in their eyes joy at his saving their dad, or relief at escaping the obligation of donating one of their own kidneys? Cyril chastised himself for such a mean and selfish thought. His mother said nothing. Della embraced him.

"Everyone out," said Paul. "I want to talk to my brother." Steve and Chuckie helped their grandmother into the corridor. Alone, Paul asked Cyril to come closer and then contemplated him. "You're an asshole," he concluded. "A sneak and an asshole. You think you can get the upper hand this way? You think I want to be in debt to you?"

Cyril stared stupidly.

"I've been a shit to you all my life. A shit. I know it. You know it. Della's been giving me hell for twenty years over it. Even ma knows it. Sometimes I actually feel bad about it. Now you're gonna be the martyr?" He snorted. "Fuck off, Cyril. I wouldn't give you one of mine."

Cyril's voice was strangled with emotion. "I've spent my life being blamed by you for something that wasn't my fault."

"So? I've spent my life suffering for something that wasn't my fault. I think you got the better deal."

"I said I'll give you a kidney and I mean it."

Paul smiled. Not his usual sour little number but an affable smile. "But the Lord will give me life everlasting, Cyril."

For a moment Cyril almost believed his brother had found faith. Was this what happened when you faced death?

The others came back in. When Paul told them his opinion of Cyril's offer no amount of argument could change his mind, and to put an end to the debate he kicked them all out saying he was tired.

They went to the cafeteria.

"It's because you're reluctant," his mother said. "He sees it. He senses it. It's in your eyes and in your voice and even in the way you stand."

Stand? How did he stand? Aware of Della and Steve and Chuckie watching, Cyril said he'd only wanted more information, was that so unreasonable, to want more information? "I'll do it. I told him I'd do it. We talked about it."

"It's too late," said his mother. "It's not a gift from the heart." She looked away and it was all Cyril could do to keep from reaching across and smacking her just as she'd smacked him.

"It's not too late," he said. "He'll come around. He has no choice."

Two days later Cyril met with the surgeon who outlined what kidney donation entailed. Apparently it was harder on the donor than the recipient. Cyril nodded. He'd heard that. They ran tests, he gave blood, he was given a strict diet, and he became depressed and resentful and afraid.

Not that it mattered. Paul continued to resist. In fact he seemed strengthened by this final act of defiance. When their mother begged him he turned his face to the wall and refused to sign the papers: no signature, no operation. Only Della respected his decision.

Yvonne had come to the hospital a number of times as well. She urged Cyril not to feel guilty. He appreciated that. He was glad she'd come. They hadn't seen much of each other since the night of her debut at the Classical Joint. She and Cyril took Della for a drink after one visit, and watching Yvonne console Della it struck Cyril that maybe she was missing her calling and that she too should have gone into nursing. Later, Yvonne said how impressed she was at Della's dignity through it all.

Cyril visited one evening before his drawing class. No one else was there and Paul was asleep. Maybe it was the drugs, but he looked more peaceful than Cyril had ever seen him, his head angled as if to look out the window at the treetops. Taking out his sketchbook, Cyril did some drawings.

"Aren't I supposed to take my clothes off?" Paul's eyes were open.

Cyril dropped his pencil.

"Lemme see."

He held the sketches up.

Paul said nothing for a long time. Then with wonder in his voice he said, "Jeez, I sure look better'n I feel." He then shocked Cyril by asking if he could have them.

"Okay."

Paul held the drawings in his hands and studied them as though memorizing the face of a long lost relative. For the next week the dialysis machine kept him alive, but it was no match for his will, for he descended doggedly, as though by choice, with a distinct air of triumph, into a coma and stayed there until he died.

At the funeral his mother, Steve, and Chuckie refused to look at Cyril much less speak to him. Only Della was civil.

೦೨   ೧೨

Over the following months Cyril and Yvonne drifted apart. He called one night and, getting no answer, he drove down to the Classical Joint. It was late, nearly eleven. Standing outside he peered through the window and saw her on stage. He paid his two dollars and went in. He had to admit that her singing had improved. She was on key and less mannered, though there were still a few smirks and rolled eyes from the audience. Looking around for a chair Cyril spotted Della. He was about to join her when the set ended and Della leapt up and applauded longer and louder and more enthusiastically than anyone else. Yvonne went straight to her and they embraced.

೦೨   ೧೨

Paul's death didn't mean Cyril never saw him again. In fact he began seeing him all too much. One night he appeared squatting like a gargoyle at the end of Cyril's bed, sucking so fiercely at a cigarette that his eyes glowed like a stoked furnace. Another night he woke from a vision of Paul duct taping barbells to his legs and pushing him off a pier, the bubbling grey water rushing up past his face while the weights dragged him down. Night after night such scenarios recurred until eventually Cyril couldn't sleep at all. It was as if Paul was waiting inside his head. The family was there too, his mother and his father and Steve and Chuckie watching with barbed wire expressions. Sleeping pills made it worse, functioning like a straitjacket that kept him helplessly at the whim of his tormenters. He paced and he drank and soon his neighbours complained about his heavy tread. The manager warned him, so Cyril started taking marathon walks around the city. More than once he was accosted by muggers, perverts, and madmen lurching from bushes. He resumed pacing indoors and the complaints also resumed. He bought a rug to muffle his footsteps but the complaints continued because by then he was moaning out loud and begging them to leave him alone.

Eventually the police arrived. Drunk, distraught, Cyril resisted, had to be restrained, and was hustled out in handcuffs. A cop put his hand on his head and, as if shoving him under water, plunged him into the back of the squad car. He spent the night in jail, was advised to seek counselling, and was back home by noon where he discovered an eviction notice waiting under his door. It was all down on record, all down in a file, right there alongside the weapons charge for having pointed that pistol at those three guys in his cab.

PART FOUR – 1995

In Which Cyril Discovers Fire

ONE

CYRIL DREAMED OF Connie smoking a cigarette in long luxurious puffs that left red lipstick on the filter. Her black bangs hung to her black eyebrows, she wore a black turtleneck sweater, black Levis, black kung fu slippers. At her elbow was a cup of black coffee, the cup white with a black cat stamped on it. They were in a jazz club. She nodded to the mutter and thump of the upright bass and watched the black saxophonist bend his knees and lean back clenching his body as though to inflate the room through the bell of the glittering brass instrument. The storming music collided with the lounging cigarette smoke: the music laughing and the smoke sullen at having been disturbed in its slumber. Sleepy people bobbed their heads. Cups and cigarettes rose and fell with mechanical regularity while the bass player, a big black man with pitted cheeks and a goatee, cursed the white guitarist. "Play something!" he shouted. The guitarist cringed. "Play something!" repeated the bassist. The guitarist sweated and his eyes rolled like a panicked cow. People in the audience laughed. Each table had a candle burning in a red glass bowl making Cyril think of a pagan cave. The guitarist finally burst into a flame that flared then vanished. No one seemed to notice. Connie leaned close and blew smoke into Cyril's mouth and he inhaled it deep into his chest and then exhaled it back into her waiting lips. She smiled and stood on the table and began to whirl like a dervish. Faster and faster she whirled, creating a wind that caught Cyril up like Dorothy and Toto and landed them outside in an alley. The club door whacked open and the bass player threw a man out. The man flapped off like a pigeon into the night. The bass player glared at Connie and Cyril and said, "Broadway Credit Clothiers—fifty short paces west of Main," then went back inside.

He woke to light outlining the curtains like a rectangular halo. The clock read 5:01 AM. Rolling onto his stomach he shoved his face into his pillow and tried going back to sleep. He wanted to rejoin the dream but it had disappeared downstream into the darkness like a raft on a river. But there was another dream. This one involved his mother and a different raft: a ghoul extending a gnarly hand for a fare to transport Cyril's mother to the far shore where fires burned and people writhed and chains snaked in the smouldering dirt.

The next time he woke he put his hands to his face and groaned and sat up. Today was his mother's funeral. He dressed slowly in the same clothes he'd worn to Paul's funeral. That had been a warm spring day as well. It occurred to him that his dad had died in the spring, and he wondered if this was some characteristic of his family to die when the days were getting longer and the grass and the flowers and the trees and the birds were all returning to life.

Father Shevchenko delivered his eulogy. "Our dear friend Helen's life was a testament to faith and fortitude. Her early years were often an ordeal, but she never stopped believing…"

Cyril stared at his feet. His shoes were shiny and his toes pinched, and he was wondering just what his mother had believed in. For all her Virgins and candles it was certainly no God Shevchenko would approve of, more like some grim trickster with bells on his toes and a slippery glint in his eye. Cyril raised his face and looked up into the canopy of maple leaves. They glowed as translucent as a mosaic of tinted glass. He shifted his head and stared straight into the sun. When he shut his eyes yellow spots lingered and he thought of his father and kept his eyes shut until the spots faded. When he opened them he blinked in confusion, for something was up there—a charcoal coloured cat lying full length along a branch like some sort of panther, and it was staring straight at Cyril as though studying him. For a moment he expected it to start talking, to stand up on its hind legs and do a bit of soft-shoe with a cane and top hat, a Cheshire cat with a message for him. He flashed on the notion that it was a message from his mother, her spirit already having reincarnated, yet his mother had hated cats, and it seemed a most unlikely form for her to take.

He was diverted by the casket being lowered into the hole. Then Gilbert's hand settled on his shoulder while with his other hand he presented the shovel which had a black ribbon tied around the shaft and a brightly polished blade. Cyril stabbed the blade into the heap of soil and poured it slowly, as though fearful of disturbing her, onto the casket battering the roses. The earthy smell of the grave was spiced by the scent of sap and grass. Steve took the shovel and did the same, then it was Chuckie's turn. Cyril peered up into the tree again but saw only leaves.

Later, he walked between the gravestones and across the lane and entered the backyard. For her sake he'd done his best to keep up the garden and now the roses and hydrangeas were in bloom, the rhubarb was spreading vast primordial leaves, and the grass was up to his ankles. He felt besieged. As for the root vegetables, the beets and turnips and parsnips and cabbage, they were on their own.

He entered the slammed-door silence of the kitchen. His mother hadn't acknowledged much less admitted that she was dying. There had been no final words, no noble last days, no truths passed on or secrets unveiled, instead she'd devoted her remaining strength to maintaining a facade of normalcy. She was bedridden, sure, but in control, as if it was her choice to lie there all morning and afternoon and evening like a lady of leisure, and if Cyril ever dared look troubled or tearful her eyes silently commanded him to control himself; after all, wasn't she? He recalled a poem about a tiger that Connie used to recite, how the animal paced its cage yet didn't turn because of the bars but because that was when and where it decided to turn, and he envied the animal—and his mother—their unbreakable spirits.

Staring out the kitchen window he watched the maples brood over the graves. Was the cat still up there? He got the opera glasses his mother used to watch funerals. He'd bought them for her at the St. Vincent de Paul as a joke, one that to his surprise and relief she liked. In fact it became an ongoing bit of comedy, a rare thing for them to share, her assuming a haughty pose and gazing upon the funerals like Madame La de Dah. He studied the tree but saw no cat. There were now three Andrachuks in the cemetery: his father, Paul, and now his mother, their graves side by side.

He went into the living room, poured himself a Ballantyne's and found himself looking at his mother's Virgin Marys. There were all kinds, plastic, metal, wood, glass, wax, stone, the one he'd brought back from Mexico which was surrounded by a halo of sea shells, and others that had haloes of crinkled plastic. He recalled Typhoon Freda back in 1962 when the power went out and the storm sent garbage cans banging down the street and the Madonnas had seemed to come alive, gleaming serenely in the writhing candlelight while the house shook and his mother prayed.

The scotch went down with a welcome burn. He refilled his glass. Steve had put the obituary in the paper, but Cyril hadn't read it, he never read obituaries, regarding it as slightly obscene and certainly bad luck. Gilbert believed the opposite, savouring obituaries, examining the deceased's picture, seeking out the cause of death, delighting in the maudlin phrasing as though it was immortal prose, laughing at Cyril's squeamishness after having grown up next to a death yard. Gilbert had even suggested Cyril do a series of drawings, maybe turn it into a coffee table book, of graves and obituaries, insisting that it would become a cult classic and sell millions. Decanting the whisky slowly into his mouth, Cyril let it seethe over his tongue.

Returning to the kitchen he looked out the back recalling the time just after the Cuban Missile Crisis that he came home from school to find a backhoe digging a massive hole in their yard. The machine operator saw Cyril's expression and jerked his thumb indicating Cyril's mother watching from the window. Cyril went up the steps and into the kitchen and demanded to know what was going on? She said don't be a simpleton, it's a bomb shelter. Apparently it didn't matter that the Soviets had withdrawn their missiles, she believed what she believed, and began explaining in a quiet tone, as if Cyril was still a child and not to be alarmed, that it was a reasonable precaution—that one could never be too cautious—because the world had gone mad before and madness was like bacteria that lived on all around them, in the soil, in the air, in their very bodies, and could erupt at any moment. She put her hand on his as she spoke and her eyes pleaded with him to believe and Cyril had nodded and said quietly, soothingly, "Okay mama, okay."

Paul had not been as indulgent. When he dropped by that evening and nearly fell in the pit he was angry. He and his mother argued and Cyril could see Paul was not only frustrated by her paranoia but humiliated by what the neighbours must be thinking. Paul took her face between his palms and forced her to look into his eyes. "We're safe," he told her, and thumbed the tears from her face. The next day he paid the backhoe driver to refill the hole.

∽ ∾

For the wake Steve had prepared roast pork with apple sauce, duck with an orange glaze, garlic meatballs, an assortment of veal, pork, and liver sausage, potato dumplings, cabbage rolls, sausage rolls, poppyseed cake, walnut cake. An impressive achievement in such a small kitchen. Steve and Marlene had recently made the sudden and unexplained move of selling their five-bedroom house and downsizing into a two-bedroom apartment, an act that neither Cyril or his mother had understood.

Yet she would have certainly approved of all the meat on the table dominating the small dining room. There could never be enough meat. In her mind animals looked like butcher's posters, sectioned into quarters and shanks and briskets. Side bacon, back bacon, all the varieties of sausage, all the organs, liver, kidney, heart, brain, tongue, tripe. Along with beef, pork, lamb, chicken, fish, duck, goose, squab, she was happy to eat goat and horse, all in compensation for the starvation years of the 1930s and 1940s.

In the living room stood a glass table with photos of Cyril's mother, father, and Paul. There was also one of the sketches Cyril had done of Paul on his deathbed, framed in mock brass. He couldn't recall having seen it on display before, not that he was often invited to Steve's.

Bottle of red wine in one hand and a bottle of white in the other, Steve draped an arm around Cyril's shoulders.

"I'm grateful to have known her." Gazing at Cyril with earnest drunk eyes, he added, "I only wish I knew my grandfather, too. Tell me about him."

It had been forty years since he'd died and Cyril didn't know what to say, more importantly he didn't know what he wanted to say, or what he was willing to share: that his father had nightmares, that he was haunted, that he was never happier than when wearing his welding mask and leaning over his bench with that acetylene torch? So many memories of his father were fading. Had Paul never told Steve anything? "He liked Laurel and Hardy," said Cyril. "And Chaplin. And Buster Keaton. All those old guys."

Hearing those names drew Father Shevchenko into the conversation. "Chaplin. *The Great Dictator*. Genius. And brave." Shevchenko smelled heavily of camphor and vodka. His long grey beard made Cyril think of a tangled root system. "Hitler wanted his head."

Steve's heavy-lidded eyes considered the priest, then he shocked both Shevchenko and Cyril with a story about the war. "Grandma told me there'd been rumours of Cossack regiments going over to the Germans. Grandpa considered defecting. She said what if they were defeated? He'd be shot as a traitor and then what about her and dad? In the end it didn't matter because he was captured and put in a camp. Then when the Krauts overran them she and hundreds of women got transported into Germany. She left dad with a neighbour. Two years in a munitions factory. Munition factories were prime targets for the Allied bombing raids. Why waste good Germans when you can stick a subhuman Slav in there, eh?"

Shevchenko exhaled.

Cyril didn't breathe at all.

"The manager's assistant was a woman, Frau Wagner." He pronounced it Vogner. "She needed a secretary, someone who could type fast and accurate. So grandma said that's me. Can you do forty words per minute? She said she could do fifty. You believe that? Hadn't typed in a year. They set her up and said type. She did sixty. That got her off the factory floor and into the office. Heat. Quiet. Flowers in a vase. Coffee, *real coffee*. She said she hadn't tasted real coffee in five years." Steve paused as if choking up. "She wept when she told me that."

Cyril observed the dramatic touch. Coffee? She never drank coffee, she was a tea drinker.

"Apparently this Frau Wagner was beautiful. But ruined. She'd lost her husband and her son. One day she couldn't talk about it and then the next she couldn't stop. She made up stories. How the boy was living in Argentina. How after the war she would meet him and they would go to the circus, because the boy loved the circus and practised magic tricks, could make cards disappear. Ten months grandma worked for her. Shared her meals, which meant she ate twice what the others did. They hated her for that but didn't dare touch her. Sometimes grandma even went to her house to work. Place was full of clocks. Grandma remembered that. Clocks. Ticking like hearts. A house full of hearts. Those were her words. A house full of hearts. When the Red Army liberated them Frau Wagner was taken away and shot."

Cyril nodded familiarly to Steve, meaning he knew the story well. In fact he was scalded. Why had she never told him? If she'd kept it from everyone he could understand, but to tell Steve?

"Incredible," said Shevchenko, eyes brimming.

Steve nodded deeply. Then turned abruptly to Cyril. "Oh yes" he said, as if just remembering. "About the will. Grandma named me executor." He shrugged implying that it only made sense. "It's what I do. Pop by the office tomorrow. Say ten. We'll sort it out. Pretty straightforward." And with that Steve slopped more wine into Cyril's glass and, discovering that the bottle was now empty and he was lapsing in his hostly duties, went off to find another.

Father Shevchenko turned his considerable attention upon Cyril and asked how he was bearing up.

Cyril performed a long exhalation bespeaking his pain.

Shevchenko nodded quickly. He sipped his drink and smoothed his beard. "Your mother told me you're a bit of an artist."

He became evasive. "Is that what she said?"

"It's God's gift."

Cyril made vague noises and wondered what she meant by a *bit* of an artist? Mockery? "I push a pencil around."

"You owe it to your talent to do more than that."

He'd read somewhere that a *talent* was a measure of ancient Roman currency. His mother had never mentioned anything to him about talent, his, hers, Paul's, anyone's, God-given or hard-won. Cyril didn't know the priest well. As a boy he'd thought of priests as unimaginative wizards who performed the same act over and over each Sunday.

Chuckie appeared with a beer in one hand and a slab of poppyseed cake in the other. Shevchenko leaned away as though preparing for an assault, a reaction that Chuckie seemed to enjoy.

"How's school, Charles?" asked Shevchenko.

"They invited me to leave."

"Why would they do that?"

Cyril detected beneath the priest's concern a hint of vindication, a hint of satisfaction at justice being served.

Chuckie was working on his PHD in Political Science. Something to do with Bolsheviks and Mensheviks, the one advocating industrial expansion and the other agrarian expansion. Cyril had looked it up. The one time he'd asked about his studies Chuckie, perhaps tired, perhaps disdainful, perhaps simply a goof, had ignored the question and talked about baseball. Cyril hadn't known whether to be insulted or bemused. Chuckie had been at his doctorate ten years and racked up forty thousand dollars in student loan debts and now worked part-time in the post office. Cyril could not deny that Chuckie had genuinely liked his grandmother, or at least found her an interesting source of information. He was always in the kitchen cross examining her about Ukraine, though never failed to end those sessions without borrowing money. In deference to the occasion, Chuckie's thinning blond hair, usually in a ponytail, was combed and his goatee trimmed.

"It's the law of the excluded middle," Chuckie explained to Shevchenko. "Black–white. Is–isn't. In–out. I, it would seem, am out." Chuckie smiled exposing a thick black grouting of poppy seeds between his teeth. He'd inherited Della's teeth, long and white, and eyes that protruded.

"I don't follow."

"I don't follow either. That's the problem. Nonconformity. By way of punishment they would fain deny me access to the means of doctoral production." Chuckie's grin widened.

"The PHD trap."

"It's a Mexican standoff. I owe them money and they owe me a doctorate."

"So you've finished your thesis?"

"I have written five hundred and thirty-five pages."

"That's a lot of pages."

"Indeed it is. Over twice the requirement."

"What do you plan to do?"

"That would be telling."

"There must be some recourse."

Chuckie's smile widened and his eyes narrowed. He

shrugged as if it was all quite simple. "Doesn't matter anyway. Funding cuts will render degrees useless. The Tower will crumble on its own."

"Well, best of luck, Charles." Shevchenko excused himself and escaped.

"How's the post office?" asked Cyril.

Chuckie seemed to enjoy that; he seemed to be having a fine old time at his grandmother's wake. "The post office is a mill for churning paper. Same way the stock exchange is a mill for churning money. But not to worry, the system unwittingly produces its own gravediggers."

"Sounds ominous."

"Depends on which side of the barrier you stand. Like you, you'll be in trouble."

Cyril waited, intrigued. He'd always found Chuckie the more interestingly erratic of his two nephews. "How so?"

"The artist draws the carpenter's chair and thus his picture is twice removed from reality. *The Republic*."

Cyril hadn't exactly read much Plato. Drive out the lying poets or something. "Is that what's coming?"

"Like an avalanche."

"Ever hear from your mother?"

He grinned. "Yesterday. Sent her regrets. She and Yvonne are doing fine down in Rio. She's nursing and Yvonne got herself a part in a Brazilian soap opera." Chuckie reached with his glass and clinked Cyril's and then went off for a refill.

∽ ∾

It was four in the afternoon when Cyril got home from the

wake. He wandered the house then out into the yard where he clipped seven yellow roses from the garden, fit them into a vase with some water and sugar, and carried them across the alley to his mother's grave. Her stone was warm from the sun. He kept his palm on the granite for a long time as if the heat was a sign of her soul's lingering presence.

He looked up at the maple tree, thinking of the cat. Maybe he hadn't seen it at all, maybe he'd imagined it. The thought disappointed him. Now he saw only leaves. He could see the appeal of watercolours to participate in all that light and colour, even though colour had never been his chief interest. What intrigued him were lines, the cracks in sidewalks and old roads, the fissures in walls and in stone, the grain of wood, the wrinkles in aging faces, the lines in the palm of a hand—lines which held the secrets of the future. Looking closely at his own skin revealed a mesh of fine lines. Hair was lines, veins and arteries were lines, as were spiderwebs and tree branches, and the thread that made up his clothes. Whenever he looked up he saw hydro lines and telephone lines, maps and charts were lines. To draw, to follow the line unwinding from a pen, was for him the most natural thing in the world, and the most exciting.

The cemetery was framed on three sides by houses and Cyril could recite the name of every owner going back forty years. He'd never told anyone, not even Gilbert, but he sometimes saw the ghost of Old Man Hunt two doors down, cutting his lawn with a steel-wheeled push mower. Hunt had survived the Battle of Vimy Ridge only to die while doing the lawn one spring morning in 1957, right in front of twelve-year-old Cyril who was raking Hunt's grass for a quarter. The old guy dropped face down in the strip of newly mown lawn as though he'd ploughed a path from the battlegrounds of France to a cemetery in Vancouver. Hunt had been a joker, always plucking nickels from kids' ears and singing Cockney songs, and for a moment Cyril had thought he was faking, especially since only minutes before he'd told him a joke about a parrot.

"Bloke goes into a pet shop. Wants a bird, see. I got this fine parrot right 'ere, says the proprietor. Bloke looks at it. Does it talk? Not yet, it's young, you can teach it. He buys it and takes it 'ome and the next morning wakes up to this croaky voice saying, *Shit it's cold, shit it's cold.* Goes into the living room and there's the parrot: *Shit it's cold.* Well this chap, 'e's very conservative, 'e is. Doesn't drink, doesn't swear, doesn't take the Lord's name in vain. Marches that bird back to the shop. Owner says no problem, next time the bird starts up you grab him around the neck and give him a good hard shake. He'll stop. Guaranteed. So the next morning our man he wakes up to the bird complaining, *Shit it's cold. Shit it's cold.* The chap's 'aving no part of this. He opens the cage and grips the parrot round the neck and gives him a good shaking about. Parrot says, *Fuck, it's windy too!*"

TWO

CYRIL HAD BEEN home from the wake nearly three hours before remembering that he had his drawing class that evening. Late, but desperate for diversion, he grabbed his stuff. Over the years students had come and gone but Cyril had remained. Novak was leaner and more saurian than ever, his grey hair long and lank, the lids of his eyes like canvas flaps. This evening he wore bare feet and sandals, black jeans, a red shirt buttoned at the cuffs and loose at the collar. Cyril arrived to find him deep in conversation with Richard.

Short, lean, with a dark beard and round metal-frame glasses over darting eyes, Richard was intensely ambitious. He'd graduated from art school—a fact concerning which he regularly reminded Cyril—and was taking Novak's class purely for the models and the feedback. Richard was big on feedback, especially giving it. He pronounced Cyril's work 'alternately erratic and cautious', and he argued with Novak—politely but adamantly—in defence of his vision. That he had a vision impressed Cyril, who wasn't sure if he himself had one. Maybe he was just too close to his own work to be able to see his own vision. Richard's vision consisted of crabs: crabs on pillows, crabs on the hoods of cars, crabs on a woman's belly, crabs falling from the sky in parachutes, crabs lurking in brassieres, crabs behind executive desks, crabs in churches preaching from altars with their claws raised in exhortation. There was no denying that they were impressive crabs, they reeked of sea and rage and occasionally of yearning. These crabs dreamed. If Cyril drew a crab it would not look like a Richard crab; he knew because he'd experimented. His crabs were good, but were they idiosyncratically him? Would someone say they were distinctly Cyril Andrachuk crabs? The question bothered him more than he cared to admit. Cyril wasn't sure he liked Richard, and it bothered him that Novak clearly liked him a lot. Their arguments were not fights but a spirited crossing of swords that seemed to exhilarate them both.

Now Novak addressed the class.

"Okay, my friends. I have worked a miracle for you. Bow your heads in gratitude. Kneel. Light candles, burn incense, give coins and virgins. For behold: Novak has done it again."

An anticipatory murmur moved through the group; Cyril's reaction was closer to dread than anticipation. Over the years Novak had arranged half a dozen group shows, only the first of which Cyril had participated in. A couple of times he'd congratulated himself on staying out of them, especially when the scorn had come pouring down like a river of mud on their heads, but the last show had been a success, young Richard had sold all his work and been approached by an agent. Novak had been courted as well. He'd been interviewed and now had his own show scheduled. Furthermore, his popularity as a teacher had soared, and instead of one session a week he now taught three.

"But not the school gallery. No, no. This time you play for keeps. This time we take the tips off our swords. This time we draw blood. At The Arena. Maybe Ms. Preston she is going senile," he admitted, referring to owner and curator Pamela Jean Preston. Last month Novak had shown her slides of their work and she'd gone for it. "She has a gap in her schedule," Novak explained. "One night. A Sunday. Not much, but maybe enough."

Richard led a round of applause and Novak bowed deeply to the left, to the right, and to the middle.

The Arena was notorious. A recent show had featured a thousand and one human teeth in all their stained and carious decay. Another show was a display of evisceration photos. Then there had been the fire-walker, some mad man who walked naked over hot coals while reciting at length from the *Epic of Gilgamesh*.

After the class, Novak caught Cyril before he could escape. He had a surprisingly strong sharp grip. "Most people you can't hold them back," he said. "All they want is a show, attention, glory, praise, look at me, look at me!" He jerked his thumb at Richard. "Like Little Big Dick there." Cyril was eager to hear criticism of Little Big Dick, that he was hollow, would soon fall on his face, and was not half the artist Cyril was. But Novak did not say that. Instead he observed that there was nothing wrong with ambition, that ambition was good, that no one got anywhere without it. "But you, you hide."

Richard, across the room, was taking note of the scene.

In a low voice Cyril said, "I'm not hiding."

Novak did not deign to argue, nor did he keep his voice down. "Hide much longer you'll rot. Like a potato in a cellar."

"We know how successful my last show was," said Cyril.

"Twenty years ago. And it wasn't your show, it was a group show. Forget it. Grow up. Accept yourself. You're good."

"Good isn't always enough."

Impatience hardened Novak's face. "Don't fuck with me. You want to fuck with yourself, fine, go into a closet and shut the door and fuck with yourself, but don't fuck with me."

Departing students skirted wide around them. Richard was the last to go, a smirk tickling the corners of his mouth.

"What are you?" demanded Novak.

Cyril stared.

"Decide. And soon."

"Okay."

But Novak hadn't finished with him. "Did you know I have a son?"

It was the first Cyril had heard.

"Twenty-five years I haven't seen him."

Cyril waited, unsure whether there was pride or lament in that statement and wondering why Novak was telling him.

"His mother called last night. Every year or so she calls. Our son, Istvan, he lives with her. He's this fat." Novak spread his arms wide. "He sits. He does nothing." Novak made a face like a toad. "His mother blames me; I blame her. Same as always. A mess. When we emigrated she was homesick. She wanted to go back. Didn't matter that in Hungary there was no meat, no milk, no coffee. Didn't matter that they lived on potatoes, that the phones were tapped, that everyone was a rat. Me, I've never been back and I never will go back. I don't go to Hungarian restaurants. I don't go to Hungarian clubs. I don't even talk to Hungarians. Fuck them. All they do is dig up the old dirt. Scratch their scabs and keep the wounds raw. I'll tell you the happiest day of my life was the morning I woke up realizing I'd begun dreaming in English. Free at last! But her, she was always talking Hungarian to him. He must know his roots! I said bullshit, roots are a ball and chain. She was horrified. It was like I spat on the cross." Novak exhaled long out his nose and contemplated the problem of his ex-wife and his lump of a son. At last he shook his head as if there was no solution. "And then there is you," he said coming to the point. "You are doublefucked. And do you know why? Because you are nostalgic for the ball and chain you never even had." Putting his palms together as though to pray, Novak rested his chin upon his fingertips and after a moment's thought he stated, "I make it simple for you: join the show or don't come back to the class."

ᔐ ᔐ

Steve sat enthroned in a black leather chair behind an oak and brass desk. Not solid oak, but plastic veneer, a piece of furniture made of particle board slapped together on an assembly line. Cyril felt a faint disappointment in his nephew and at the same time grim satisfaction. He evaluated the sloppy paint job on the office walls: beige colliding like a storm surge against a white ceiling, not to mention the drips and roller marks. Cyril had been running his own painting business for twenty years. Interesting how Steve hadn't offered him the work; he was slighted though at the same time relieved.

Bad paint job aside, the walls testified to Steve's success. There was his university diploma, his law school diploma, wedding photos, honeymoon-on-Kauai photos, pictures of Courtenay and Candace at birth, one, two, three, and four years of age. There were pictures of Steve and Marlene grinning beneath the Eiffel Tower and in Saint Peter's Square. There were pictures from their various cruises, including one of Steve cradling a bottle of Dom Castro port, 1953, and, in the centre of them all, one where he had his arm around the shoulders of Graham Kerr, *The Galloping Gourmet*. Yet what spooked Cyril were the photographs of Cyril himself. He and Steve rarely saw each other more than twice a year, at Christmas and Easter, but there he was, uncle Cyril, as a kid, as a teen, in his twenties. He should have been touched; in fact he felt as though he'd been spied upon.

Cyril remembered Steve eating flies from the window ledge. The flies had always been alive—fresh meat only for him. Since then his interest in cuisine had flourished.

The office was in a bright new building on Vancouver's west side, but somewhat tainted by the fact that Steve's one window looked across an alley at a water-stained apartment with sagging balconies. Still, Steve's clothes were impeccable, his charcoal suit enlivened by fine silver stripes and his cerise tie charged by bolts of silver lightning. As for his hair, it was styled short and dyed blond and oiled straight back, while his ear gleamed with a red stud. Cyril wore jeans. They were fairly new, not yet faded and thereby demoted to work pants. His shirt was grass-green, button-down, short-sleeved. He wore no watch, no ring.

"Grandma and I were always close," Steve said. "But toward the end we really talked. She really confided in me."

Cyril acknowledged the profound depths of Steve's relationship with his grandmother even though, *frau* Vogner story aside, he suspected it was Steve who'd done all the confiding, Cyril's mother never the sort to bare her soul—at least she'd never bared much of it to him.

On the desk were a computer and some papers, a champagne flute full of pens and pencils and a red ceramic bowl heaped with black liquorice. Steve pushed the bowl forward.

Cyril declined.

Chuckie, comatose until now, woke and heaved himself forward with a grunt and pawed up a handful then flumped back into his chair. He wore stained sweatpants and a stained baseball shirt and a grubby ponytail. Slapping the entire handful of liquorice into his mouth he chewed loudly and wetly then dug a wad from a tooth and examined it before sucking it from his finger and resuming his masticating. Steve glanced at Cyril as though to bond over such lamentable manners. Cyril opted for an expression of innocent neutrality. After all, both boys had always regarded their uncle as a chump.

Cyril looked again at the photographs. Steve followed his gaze. "Grandma gave me the ones of you."

"I wondered."

"I think she kind of wished you'd have drawn her."

Cyril was frankly surprised.

"She told me," said Steve. "All grandpa's stuff but never her. I don't know," he added quickly, seeing where this was going and switching tracks before it was too late, "just what she mentioned." He shrugged.

Connie and Cyril had once gone into a photo exhibit titled *Portraits of Old Europe*. Big black and white images of refugees plodding along dirt roads, aristocrats in decayed splendour, peasants in fields, gypsies in covered wagons. Connie had asked if he ever drew his mother? He said she wouldn't let him. But he'd never asked, he'd have been afraid to. All those statues of the Virgin, did he draw those? He hesitated and said sometimes. But she saw through him. Liar. Yet she was smiling. Then why did you ask? Because I like to see you work without a script.

Steve picked up a document and passed it across to Cyril. "The will. All pretty simple."

Pushing himself up from the depths of the leather chair, Cyril took the papers then sank back down with the seat exhaling beneath him. *Last Will and Testament. Helen Mary Teresa Andrachuk.* He stared at the print, the thick bold lettering, the smooth white paper. Was he supposed to read it all right then and there? He paged through, noting titles and clauses and subclauses marked with Roman numerals. V was five, X was ten, and C was a hundred. Or was C fifty and L a hundred? Aware of Steve and Chuckie watching him he adopted a discerning expression.

Steve paged through his own copy and repeated that it was all fairly straightforward, and for the next half hour he talked while Chuckie began to snore.

Cyril did his best to follow all the legalese, the pursuants and heretofores, and finally blurted: "Who gets the house?"

"Well, you. Just like I've been saying."

Cyril waited for just what he hadn't been saying.

"Chuck and I get twenty-five thousand cash and everything else is yours." His clean-shaven face was wide and smooth and open while his cheeks glowed with a purplish flush. "Though," he cautioned, "this is all contingent upon—" he coughed "—a psychiatric evaluation."

Cyril moved back through the phrase with caution, like a tightrope walker going in reverse. Evaluation. Psychiatric. Contingent.

Chuckie was sitting forward now while Steve sat with his fingers on the edge of his desk as if about to play a piano—or leap back in case uncle Cyril got violent.

"Psychiatric evaluation?"

Steve shrugged at a hard but inescapable fact.

"I go to a shrink?"

"That you, yes, well—" Steve swayed his head side-to-side as if to say that was a bit blunt. "That you discuss a few things and get the thumbs up. Either that or I take control of the house." He tagged this last part on as though it was scarcely worth mentioning.

"You get the house."

Steve backtracked. "Take control of the house. But you'd live in it. If you want."

"But you'd own it."

Steve had no choice but to nod at his uncle's lamentably simplistic phrasing. "In effect."

Cyril gripped his knees to steady himself. See a shrink or Steve got his mother's estate. He looked at Chuckie who pretended to be absorbed by the state of his fingernails. Cyril understood: his breakdown. He preferred to think of it as his lapse, his episode, his brief bad patch due to guilt over his brother's death. Others saw it more bluntly: it was a breakdown.

"It's just that grandma was concerned," said Steve. "The

house is worth a lot and you have to be careful these days. Real estate is very turbulent."

Cyril envisioned a grim panel of experts listening to Steve and Chuckie describe their uncle's erratic mental state. "Sure. Of course."

"And there's that business with the gun," said Steve.

"That was self-defence," said Cyril. "There were three of them. And anyway, it was twenty years ago."

Steve was nodding. "Absolutely. No doubt. But actually I meant the other business." Steve consulted some papers. "Darrel Stavrik. There's no police record, but grandma, well, she told me about it. And hey, believe me, if you fired a few shots at the guy I'm sure he earned it." Steve put up his hands as if to say far be it from him to question the judgement of his uncle Cyril. "I mean, I don't know, I wasn't there, but grandma felt it prudent to fill me in."

So Darrel had told her what had happened and she'd never in all those years confronted Cyril about it. What self-control. What reserve. The will was her revenge, served up as cold as her very own grave. He congratulated her on such impressive patience. Well played, ma, well played. Cyril experienced an epiphany: she found greater satisfaction in being the martyr than being happy, so collected icons and never again tried to find another man after Darrel.

Steve hurried on to another point, explaining what uncle Cyril-the-house-painter could not be expected to grasp, the fragility of financial markets, worldwide recession, political upheaval, flux and ferment, the mounting frenzy at the approach of the millennium. "And right here at home," he said, as if the barbarians were at the gate. "There's fraud to be wary of. Do you have call display? No?" He winced at the pain caused by such a dangerous state of affairs, as if dear uncle Cyril was living in a mine field. "I have call display. Chucko has call display. I think it's prudent. You should really get on that ASAP. In fact, I'm going to arrange it for you myself." He made a note on his blotter and underlined it twice. "Telephone fraud perpetrated on senior citizens is up three hundred and twenty percent."

"Senior citizen? I'm fifty!"

"Sure. Of course. I didn't mean anything. Only you're wise to be prepared. They know all the angles, these guys. And it's not guys, usually it's women. Believe me, when the day comes, I'll want Courtenay and Candace there looking out for me. Right now that's what Chucko and I are doing for you. Just like grandma wished." He raised his eyebrows in an innocent expression and then exhaled a long breath and stood, jingling his keys like bells in his pockets signalling that it was time for Cyril to go. Eager to escape, Cyril stood as well, noting again the photos of himself on the wall: him smiling in the sun, him with his hands on his hips ready to take on the world. No, he'd never drawn his mother.

THREE

CYRIL LEFT STEVE'S office with a copy of the will, the name of the psychiatrist, and the date of the first of five appointments, a week Friday, eleven days from now. *Just as grandma wished…* The words stood as black as bruises. Still, it was a spring day and he'd escaped his nephews even if more torment awaited. How much happier life had been as a child, the days longer, the sun warmer, the sky brighter, the horizon wide and clear and inviting. At the age of fifty he seemed to have crested a hill, except the view was not a pleasing panorama but a low dark forest of withered trees that he had no choice but to enter and from which, he knew, he'd never depart.

Passing Chuckie's van he glanced in at a slew of textbooks and papers and magazines and Styrofoam coffee cups, as well as a midden of torn and twisted tickets from the racetrack. Farther along the street was a London Drugs. He entered and found the Aspirin. He really wanted codeine, but the over-the-counter type had caffeine and he did not want to stay awake; he wanted to escape, to sleep, to dive down into the mud and stay there for a year or two. En route to the check-out he saw a rack of Do-It-Yourself booklets. *Do-It-Yourself Divorce Guide, Do-It-Yourself Tax Guide, Do-It-Yourself Will Guide*. He was tempted to take the one on wills. Otherwise, if he croaked—and given the way he felt that seemed imminent—Chuckie and Steve would get everything, or whatever he had, which, if he didn't do something soon might not be much. Were they that desperate, that greedy? He decided that the best plan was to deal with this psychiatrist and then sell the house and blow the money. Maybe buy a yacht and sink it, or fund an orphanage in Ukraine. Either way, use it all up and leave Steve and Chuckie zip...maybe a note and his mother's collection of icons. He grabbed the *Do-It-Yourself Will Guide* and headed for the checkout.

The cashier was a young woman with pale skin, black hair, a ring in her lower lip, another in her eyebrow, and too many to count in her ears. She yawned and looked through him. What with his receding hair and advancing years he'd begun to sense that he was dissolving, that he was becoming transparent, no more substantial than smoke—the smoke not of a blaze but of a dying fire—and that by the time he was sixty he'd be a ghost. As he went out the door he wondered if that meant he'd be able to walk through walls.

∽ ∾

After an evening attempting to read and comprehend the will, Cyril understood that he needed a lawyer, someone on his side. Opening the Yellow Pages he discovered that there were twenty pages devoted to lawyers. *Personal Injury. Accident Recovery*

Settlement. Injured—We're on your side! Don't Settle for Less. Breathalyzers Can Be Wrong! Whiplash. Slips & Falls. Conspiracies. Civil Litigation. Wills & Estates. Everyone, it seemed, was on his side. The ads showed the sincere and earnest faces of the men and women eager to leap to his defence. He found Steve's ad: Steven Andrachuk: *Integrity.* His face in three-quarter view, head high, gaze long. No ad mentioned fees.

He was wading through this crowd of power-suited knight errants when Gilbert arrived bearing photos. He opened an envelope fat with shots of his eight-year-old granddaughter Savannah. There she was at her first dive meet, slim and earnest as a soldier in her blue and white striped Dolphins swimsuit, poised at the end of the springboard. Then she was in the air, arms high. Then she was entering the water. Perfect. An arrow piercing her own reflection.

"That's great," said Cyril, envious. He'd never thought much about having kids and now it seemed a terrible lapse. How had he gotten so old and so alone?

"It is," said Gilbert, a fierce and adoring expression on his face as he arranged the photos.

Cyril saw that more compliments were due. "She's pretty."

"She is."

She'd done well in school. "And bright."

"Sky's the limit with this one." Gilbert had five older granddaughters who, caught in the throes of adolescence, had forgotten he even existed. "Girls," he said wearily, as though the Sisyphean burden of their upbringing was his alone.

Cyril couldn't recall which of Gilbert's four daughters by three wives was mother to Savannah. "Girls," he agreed, though could only imagine.

Eventually Gilbert slid the snaps back into their envelope and noticed the Yellow Pages and asked the obvious question. When Cyril admitted that he was thinking of challenging the will Gilbert was intrigued. The hint of drama brought a glow to his complexion. "Why? She cut you out?"

Cyril explained.

"Let's have a look."

Though reluctant he was also desperate. And the fact was that in Gilbert's decades of driving taxi he'd devoted his time to reading *The Wall Street Journal*, *Barrons*, *Fortune 500*, *The Economist*, and tomes on finance, self-empowerment, and law, most especially the rules governing estates. As he skimmed the will he frowned and he nodded and ran his hand through his hair. Gilbert's hair was still as thick as ever, and still as dark as a slab of tar because he'd been dousing it with dye for decades.

"Did you discuss the will with her?"

His mother had talked mostly about Kiev, which was sometimes in Poland and sometimes in Ukraine, which was sometimes in Russia and sometimes independent. "We talked about everything but the will." Bracing himself for the worst, he asked how bad it was.

"Well, what with your notorious record, they kind of have you against a wall and over a barrel."

That wasn't what Cyril wanted to hear.

"It says psychiatric evaluation," observed Gilbert, "but it doesn't name any one particular psychiatrist. Meaning you can choose."

"You think?"

"I'd want to take as much control as possible. Do some research," he suggested, and shoved the Yellow Pages forward.

"I don't know," said Cyril, exhausted by the very prospect of lawyers and psychiatrists. "Maybe I should just walk away. It's only a house."

"It's only a half a million dollars."

"Still..." While his history with weapons might suggest otherwise, he tended to cringe from conflict.

"Let me check my Rolodex." Gilbert's Rolodex was the cumulative result of thirty years of driving, in other words, thirty years of cross-examining people. *Did they get a flu shot? No, why not? You think they're a scam? Soy products? Oil futures? Venture capital? Biofuels? Electric cars? The tar sands? Wind energy? Solar panels? Bullion? The Yen? The Deutschmark? How about these waste-to-energy burners the city is pushing, thumbs up or down? Is that right, and you're a chemical engineer. Interesting. You have a card?*

"So we can call around?"

Gilbert looked at him with something between exasperation and amazement. Cyril knew Gilbert thought he was a simpleton when it came to business. That Gilbert was staggering under the load of three alimonies and now lived in a one-room apartment while Cyril was modestly secure did not alter his opinion. For years Gilbert had been offering financial advice on how Cyril should run his painting business, so felt entitled to take some credit for its success, such as it was. "Of course you can call around. You don't think psychiatrists need your business? I believe this is where you can be what the pundits are pleased to term *proactive* and take some control."

"I think Steve's scamming me."

There was that look again. Was there ever such a naif as Cyril? "Of course he's scamming you. He's a lawyer. It's part of their code of ethics."

"The thing is, I don't want to fight. I don't need the money. Not really. I mean I can use it but I can get by."

Gilbert was slack-jawed. "What are you, a monk? People can get by on Welfare, people can get by picking bottles from the trash. You think they're happy? You think they're fulfilled? Everyone needs money. That's a fact of life. That's the difference between thriving and subsisting. You don't want the dough fine, give it to beggars, donate it to an orphanage, hand it to the SPCA, whatever, but you can use it, and maybe most important of all you'd be keeping it out of Steve's sticky little mitt. And what about the principle? You grew up in this place, you have more right to it than Steve or that Commie reject brother of his." He gestured around as though the house was not a two-bedroom box overdue for a new roof and new wiring, but an architect-designed heritage estate gilded with history.

"Hey. I'm not totally naive," said Cyril. "Even if Steve sold it tomorrow I know damn well I'm entitled to half no matter what some shrink says."

"True enough," admitted Gilbert. "And lawyers are expensive. Even if you fought and won, legal fees could eat up every cent you gained. I should've gone into law. I'm a natural. So what're you gonna do?"

༄ ༄

Cyril didn't know what he was going to do, and he was saved from obsessing about it when the phone rang that afternoon with someone seeking a painter. He hadn't worked in three months. Desperate for diversion—though careful not to sound hungry—he said he could maybe find half an hour to come over and give an estimate. The address was nearby, so close in fact that he could walk. It was a hot, hazy day and when he headed out the door he felt as though he hadn't walked in years. The sidewalk felt foreign under his heels, and he remembered how as a kid he used to pay so much attention to sidewalks with their various textures, some smooth, some mottled, the grass and weeds jutting through the cracks, the date stamped at the kerb. Hands in his pockets and shoulders slack he took his time, his head mercifully empty. Yet as soon as he reached thirty-fifth he perked up because he knew whose house it was—whose house it somehow had to be—and checked the addresses, counting down as he approached. Yes. There. Connie's place. It had aged of course, looking small amid the tree-sized shrubs. He halted, sick, excited. Could it be her, there, now, waiting? But it had been a male voice on the phone. Her father? Cyril had never met her father, and anyway the voice had been too young, unless it was her husband... Of course it was her husband. Maybe her folks had died and she'd inherited the house and was up here trying to sell it. Likely she wanted to give it a face-lift then flip it. Standard procedure. Cyril had done dozens. In dread and anticipation he went up the walk and up the steps—wide, deep, in need of repair—to the porch, also wide, deep and in need of repair. Before he could knock the door swung inward. The screen door was so blackened with age it obscured the face on the other side. He waited, pulse thumping thick in his throat.

"Mr. Andrachuk I presume." The screen door opened revealing a guy his own age in a dark blue suit, red spiked hair, straight nose, brilliant blue eyes, and a severely trimmed goatee. "John Boston." Cyril shook John Boston's hand, noting the gold watch and the gold wedding band. "Entre and come on in." He stepped back and held the door wide enough for Cyril to pass, which was when he noticed that the man had a club foot, that one shoe had a three-inch sole and a snub toe. Cyril noticed this all in an instant, even as he was doing his best to not notice it, making a performance of gazing innocently around the foyer and living room.

The place was empty. He recognized the carved pineapple newel post at the foot of the stairs and looked up as if half expecting and half dreading Connie to appear—surprise, surprise, gotcha—but she did not appear, and he was relieved. "I'd offer you a chair but there ain't one," said Boston in a mock drawl.

"That's okay."

Discoloured rectangles—the ghosts of pictures past—darkened the walls above the wainscotting.

"You alright there, buddy? Lookin' a little pale."

"Are you the realtor or owner?" asked Cyril.

"My wife inherited it."

So. Cyril imagined Connie's life with this guy. What was he, producer, agent, entertainment lawyer? His teeth looked bleached, his haircut expensive, and a waft of cologne hovered— the aura of success. On the belt of his pleated pants hung a beeper. Cyril avoided looking at his shoe. Scenarios flew fast-forward through his mind regarding his foot. Birth defect? Injury? Had Connie married him out of pity? Or was he a jackal, a hunter, doubly ambitious due to his defect, and Connie the trophy proving he was not merely equal but superior. Cyril grew bold. "She grew up here?"

"Here? Naw. Calgary. Her parents picked it up a couple of years back. You know, enough already with the forty below winters. Time to retire to Lotus Land. Then they went and died before it could happen."

"I'm sorry," said Cyril.

"Hey. It is what it is."

Cyril nodded. A man with a club foot knew more than enough about disappointment. "I had a friend when I was a kid. She lived here."

"No shit." Boston gazed around re-evaluating the house.

"Long time ago."

"Cool." He clapped his hands once meaning that while nothing would tickle him more than a long meander down memory lane it was time to get down to business. "We want to move in. Want the whole place done. Top to bottom. Inside and out. You got a crew? How's your schedule? We want to get rocking."

"Schedule's good."

"Right on. Just to let you know I am talking to other contractors."

"Of course."

Boston produced a card, holding it slotted between his middle and index fingers, a rich and glossy red with raised black lettering. B.E.I. Boston Energy Inc. "Listen, I gotta jump. Take a look around and get back to me tonight. Cost. Time. Or is that too hop-hop?"

"No. No problem at all."

"The best paint. None of that Chinese shit."

Cyril wasn't familiar with Chinese paint.

Boston clapped him on the shoulder, shook his hand again, held out a key, then headed for the door with a surprisingly smooth stride. Had he practiced back and forth in front of a mirror? Worked with a personal trainer? "Lock up then put it through the slot." And with that, John Boston of Boston Energy Inc. was going down the steps, no clump and bump but quiet as anything, and Cyril was alone in Connie's old house.

Late afternoon sun slanted through two small stained glass windows with tulip designs in green and yellow. He stood so still that he could watch the coloured shapes crawl as slowly as sea creatures across the floor. Shutting his eyes he listened, trying to hear the echo of Connie's voice, feel the echo of her presence. He wandered into the kitchen, onto the back porch, observed the remnants of an extensive garden, peeked into the bathroom, then, at the foot of the stairs, recalled standing on this same spot all those years ago and wondered at the time that had passed and what he had done with his life, a question that seemed to be recurring a lot lately. He climbed the steps. At the top the air smelled trapped, not simply hot and stale but troubled, as though haunted by unresolved desire, and he imagined unhappy ghosts—were there any other kind—drifting along the corridor, dragging their chains like Jacob Marley. He faced the door. Thirty-three years had passed since the last time he'd stood here. He held his breath and listened, imagining her on the other side of the door biting her lip trying not to laugh, waiting with one of her swords.

He gave his head a shake and went down the steps and out the door. Before locking it he could not resist putting his face to the glass and peering through. No, Connie was not standing at the top of the stairs wondering where he'd gone. He slid the key through the slot and heard it clatter. When he got home he left John Boston a message saying he couldn't take the job.

ༀ ༀ

"Bernard Borgland," said Gilbert on the phone. He spelled it out, "B as in budgie, 'o' as in ornithology, 'r' as in raven, 'g' as in goshawk, 'l' as in lapwing, 'a' as in abracadabra, 'n' as in nut-job, 'd' as in dodo. My advice, my friend, should you decide to heed it, is to phone him, ASAP pronto. He's a good man. Moral fibre, all that noble stuff. Rare in these decadent times." Cyril wrote the name and number in the corner of the sketch he was making of an orange with a fork stuck in it. "He's waiting to hear from you."

Cyril panicked. "What did you tell him?"

"Nothing you haven't told me."

Cyril tried recalling what he had told him.

"Towhees and goldfinches at the feeder. And there, the grosbeaks are back! Gotta get my camera." Gilbert hung up.

Cyril stepped onto the porch and watched three limos follow a hearse up the cemetery roadway in a stately progress between the concrete angels, the pitted Madonnas, and mossy pillars. He thought of his mother watching this. No opera lover attended *Carmen* more rapturously than his mother watched these death processions. "The coffin was all silver and brass and I don't know what," she would say. "So many roses like you never saw. And lilies. Heaps. I opened the window and I could smell them. Mourners, maybe two hundred. They cried—and they *meant* it. I can always tell when they mean it."

The affair underway right now was small, about twenty people. The gravediggers Ron and Derrick stood dutifully to attention by the shed. Cyril wondered whether their views on mortality were grim or optimistic, or had the simple fact of repetition—grave after grave, hole after hole, dug up and filled in—drained the metaphysical angst from funerals and made the entire business mundane? Living across from a cemetery hadn't done his mother any good. She'd escaped the killing fields of Eastern Europe only to come here and be reminded every day of death.

There had been a bit on the news the other day about mass graves from World War Two discovered in Poland. The report said they were still finding cannons abandoned by Napoleon's army on the retreat from Moscow. The entire region was a graveyard. When he was a kid, Eastern Europe had been behind The Iron Curtain. He'd look at the curtains over their windows and imagine them made of iron, a steel mesh of chain link dividing the grim grey lands of Eastern Europe from the clear clean lands of the The West where the sun shone and the people smiled and the future was bright and prosperous. In his mind Eastern Europe was backward and brutal and smelled of boiled cabbage. Even the names were alien, not at all familiar and British, not at all Canadian: Czechoslovakia, Latvia, Lithuania, Estonia, Romania, Bulgaria, Moldavia, Ukraine. All those z's and v's and k's. Slovenians and Slovaks living in cities like Bratislava, Zagreb, and Kiev, the sheds and stalls of Europe, the barns and cellars. The only thing more bleak than Eastern Europe was the USSR, vast and medieval, where parents ate their young and pigs fed on the bones. His mother had hated the Russians as much as she hated the Germans: two walls of a vice crushing Ukraine in between.

Turning from the window, Cyril wondered if he should call this Borgland or just forget the entire business? Let Steve sell the house or knock it down and build something more profitable. The lot was too small for one of those suburban mansions but it could fit a Vancouver Special, one shoe box on top of another, two rental incomes from people who'd know nothing and care nothing of the house that had been demolished or the family that had lived in it.

His father had done a lot of work on the place. He'd built Paul's bedroom downstairs, done the flooring, the panelling, the ceiling, the cupboards, everything. He'd laid the carpet in the living room, even put a new roof on one spring. He'd let Cyril climb the ladder and sit with him up there in the sky, looking out over the world, all the way to the mountains.

Cyril was tempted to get the ladder and climb up onto the roof and try to relive the moment. Instead, he got into his van and drove west where more trees grew, more sun shone, and even the alleys were paved and the trash cans shiny and dent free. Steve lived on the west side. Gilbert had lived there as well until divorce number three forced him to sell at a crippling loss and retreat to ignominious exile—Gilbert's own phrase—in an aging bachelor suite off Kingsway, in the faceless wastes beyond East Vancouver in Burnaby.

West Broadway took Cyril past Steve's office—where he nearly veered off the road—for there were Gilbert and Steve in the entrance to the building: laughing. Steve with his big grin, hands in his slacks pockets—did Cyril detect or only imagine the motion of Steve jingling his keys as though his balls were just so big they demanded to be rung like bells?—wearing a white shirt and red tie. Gilbert wore one of those safari shirts with all the pockets, and of course his fedora. Gilbert reached out to clap Steve on the shoulder then they shook hands as though sealing a contract. Fists tight to the wheel, Cyril continued on by. Loop the block? And if they spotted him? He didn't care. He wrenched the wheel and booted it down to the first intersection, then went right again, and a third time, until he was back at Broadway waiting to rejoin the traffic which had suddenly become bumper to bumper in a conspiracy to delay him so that by the time he made his second pass Steve and Gilbert were gone.

Suspicion twisted his guts. Not knowing what else to do he kept driving and ended up at the beaches, Jericho, Locarno, Spanish Banks, where the late May crowds were already frolicking in the hot spring sun. He parked and watched, yet volleyball games and frisbee throwers couldn't divert him from the image of Gilbert and Steve laughing like pals, buddies— conspirators. Could they have run into each other accidentally, Gilbert on his way past just as Steve happened to emerge from the office, or were they concluding a meeting?

Sailboats tilted this way and that in a silent regatta. Freighters sat as if welded to the sheet metal sea while off to the right stood the city, silver and grey, a glare of sunlight flaring on the imperious glass and metal. Cyril leaned out the window and stared into the sun for a full minute and then shut his eyes and rested his head on the steering wheel and took comfort in the after-image flame that hovered like a visiting spirit.

FOUR

KINGSWAY ANGLED LIKE an appendix scar across the belly of the city. Cyril drove slowly, trying to hit the red lights, hoping to run into a traffic jam that would cause him to miss his appointment with Bernard Borgland altogether. He passed a desolation of strip malls, the coloured plastic pennants fluttering above the car dealerships, making them appear all the more shabby and desperate. There was the dark brick vault of the old Technocracy building. He remembered houses along here, the remnants of an orchard, the interurban trolley with its oak-trimmed cars.

Borgland's office was around the back of a drab old house on a drab grey street built in the black-and-white TV era of the 1950s. Who ran a business from a basement nowadays? Dope dealers? Tupperware salesmen? Cyril recalled a dentist he'd gone to as a kid whose torture chamber was in an old house with warped linoleum floors, peeling wallpaper, battered wain-scotting, and a ceiling draped in chains of cobweb. An office should be in an office building, that is if it was a real office, occupied by a real professional. The cement steps leading down to the door were painted red, a weird and ominous colour choice. What was this Borgland up to? Cyril had decided that he didn't care about the will, that he was ready to let Steve have control of the house, that he was not about to engage in some legal battle much less undergo a series of five psychiatric sessions with some stranger, however well or ill qualified to evaluate him. No. Forget it. As he'd told Gilbert, he didn't need the money, though of course he could use it, who couldn't, but that was hardly the point because no matter how you looked at it the whole thing stank. So why was he here at the top of these red steps? The only answer he could give himself was curiosity—maybe a perverse curiosity, maybe innocent curiosity—to see the guy's face, to hear what he might ask, to hear what he himself would say in response to whatever it was the guy might ask. Just to have a look. Who, after all, could resist having a look when it was you who were being looked at? And of course he could walk out any time he so pleased, simply stand up and flip the guy the finger, or wave, or shake his hand, say excuse me, whatever he wanted, and stroll on out.

So he took a deep breath and descended those red steps. At the bottom he was confronted by a door of yellow cedar varnished to a high gloss in the middle of which were brass theatre masks, tragedy and comedy, each with its own knocker. A test? Choose Mr. Sad and you revealed your inner desolation? Opt for Mr. Smiley and you were hiding it? He solved the dilemma by taking one knocker in each hand and rapping them both. The door swung open revealing an impressively tall though disturbingly young man.

"Cyril." He spoke warmly as though it was a much antici-pated reunion.

They shook hands, Cyril noting the slender wrist, long fingers, perfect pink nails, and delicate skin of a guy who'd never gripped a hammer or a paint brush much less known the bark-coarse texture of a callus on his own palm. Borgland looked thirty, tops. On the phone he'd sounded so much older. How could Cyril be evaluated by a boy? How could he take counselling from a kid? Bernard Borgland's complexion was so smooth and hairless it was almost raw—a soft breeze could abrade it—while his chestnut hair was so curled and bouncy he must surely have visited a salon. He did, however, wear a reassuringly conservative charcoal suit.

"You opted for compromise and balance," said Borgland, nodding to the knockers. "That's good. That's healthy. Come in, come in."

Cyril tried not to flinch when he spotted a milky-eyed Dober-man regarding him like a blind seer gauging the state of his soul.

In spite of being below ground level the office was surpris-ingly bright and airy, with potted bamboo, pine panelling, a varnished fir floor, and rattan furniture. On the walls were framed photos of tropical vistas, beaches, reefs, palms, and an undersea shot of a school of black and yellow fish with long ele-gant gown-like fins. There was no couch, which was a relief. The idea of lying down had been worrying him; it would make him feel even more vulnerable than he already did. Borgland directed him to a wicker chair which creaked as he settled in. How many others had sat here weeping as they confessed their misery? Trying not to fidget, he positioned his hands palm upward on his thighs as though meditating, except that instead of calming him the sight of his upturned mitts made him think of small dead animals with their legs in the air. He moved his fingers and that made him think the animals were still twitching. He turned them over so that they rested palm down, except now they resembled crabs. It occurred to him that he had absolutely no control over his mind. All of three minutes he'd been here and he was exhausted. Incense burning in a bowl emitted tart sweet smoke, a clock ticked, the Doberman exhaled like a walrus.

"Do you mind dogs?"

"Dogs are fine."

"Some people find Sigmund disturbing," said Borgland. "If he bothers you I can send him out."

"No, no," he lied, unwilling to admit that at the age of five he'd been humped by a Doberman and that to this day they spooked him. It had been an enormous beast with a spiked collar, and it had crossed its paws around little Cyril's shin and humped his leg, growling every time he'd tried pulling away. He noted the eerily glutinous eyes of Borgland's dog.

"Cataracts."

Cyril nodded. He'd heard that owning a dog was supposed to calm you down and make you feel involved, though it seemed to him that resorting to an animal for companionship was the depth of desperation. His mother said there were no dogs or cats during the war because they'd all been eaten. Like stringy veal, she'd added.

"Let me tell you a little about my approach," Borgland was saying. "That is, my approaches, because I have a range. I'm not strictly a Jungian, but I do think that some of his views are valid. Are you familiar with Carl Jung, Cyril?"

"Symbols have more than one meaning," he said, impressed at himself for remembering. Borgland was genuinely pleased, and Cyril was proud and at the same time indignant that Borgland should be so surprised. Did he look like such an ignorant labourer? "Exactly. Do you dream?" His tone implied that dreaming was a decision, that on a given night you might decide to do a bit of dreaming while on another you might opt to give it a miss.

"I dream. Yes."

"The ancient Greeks called dreams the Thousand Sons of Hypnos. Hypnos being the god of sleep. He'd send dreams to deliver messages to mortals."

Cyril discovered that his hands had clenched themselves into fists. He forced them open and pressed them flat to his knees.

"The brain is like a forest," Borgland continued, "a forest that is self-aware. And that self-awareness actually influences how it functions and how it grows. Follow the same paths through the forest and they widen and become roads, and those roads become harder to avoid. In fact, they become habitual routes. Ruts, if you will. This occurs in both the conscious and unconscious mind. Unresolved fears breed recurrent dreams, and so a cycle develops, a potentially undesirable cycle."

Cyril flashed on a picture he might draw, of a head or a skull dense with a thicket of bamboo sprouting from the nostrils and eye sockets and ears. "Okay, I get it."

Borgland smiled. He had a habit of stroking his clean-shaven chin as if he had a goatee. Maybe he wanted a goatee but couldn't yet grow one. "So you understand that we're doing a psychological profile."

"Got it."

"So let's begin at the beginning. Why do you think you're here, Cyril?"

He could accuse Steve of being a conman and manipulator, but would appear angry and vindictive. Or he could say this was his mother's revenge, but would appear paranoid. "They think I'm unstable."

"They?"

"My mother and my nephew."

"And what do you think?"

"I think I'm as stable as the next guy."

"Do you?" Borgland's tone was that of a benevolent teacher offering a wayward though essentially good-hearted student a second chance to come clean and tell the truth.

Cyril forced himself to breathe evenly and meet Borgland's gaze. He spoke in a measured tone, "Yes."

"Okay."

Cyril permitted himself to look around, noting again all the bamboo and thinking he'd like some in his yard even if it might not be his yard for long. In hot countries bamboo grew two feet a day, an inch an hour. Yes, he should get some bamboo, a hedge tall enough to block out the cemetery. It struck Cyril as utterly revolutionary that he could block out the cemetery and look out the kitchen window and see bamboo instead of graves, bamboo full of birds, bamboo rustling in the breeze. If he could keep control of the house he could sell it and then move somewhere with whole jungles of bamboo.

Borgland politely cleared his throat. "Do you still have nightmares about your brother Paul?"

Cyril's heart lurched. He felt himself sinking into a swamp and feared he'd made a grave error in coming. "No."

"No?"

Cyril shook his head.

"No nightmares?"

"Not really."

"So sometimes?"

Cyril's fists were locked as tight as knots; he forced them flat to his thighs. "I understand what he went through. He was traumatized. He was angry. And he was small. His growth was stunted. He had brittle bones, bad teeth."

"Did you love him?"

"I was afraid of him."

"Because he tortured you."

Cyril balked at the word. He tried to appear relaxed and reasonable. "All brothers fight."

Borgland picked up a pencil and was about to write on a pad when he paused and looked enquiringly at Cyril. "It won't bother you if I make a few notes now and then?"

"No," lied Cyril.

"You didn't feel the need of a therapist after your breakdown?"

Breakdown. It made him think of a car, dead on the side of the road. Okay, he'd skidded a bit, lost control on a curve—yet only once, and only for an instant—it had been a stressful time and afterwards he'd straightened out and carried on. "My brother had it tough. It wasn't fair what he lived through."

"The famine and then the war," said Borgland. "Your family was caught up in terrible events. You were fortunate to escape them." Consulting the file on his desk, Borgland put his fingertips together. "What do you remember about your father?"

"He smelled like metal."

"Was that good?"

"It was him."

"Did he hit you?"

"The old man? No."

"Never?" Borgland maintained eye contact.

"Not that I recall."

"So it's possible. It's common to block out traumatic memories."

"No. He wasn't violent. He didn't even shout."

"Are you angry at having to be here?"

Of course he was angry at having to be here, even if he could walk out any time he wanted. He forced himself to take a couple of low slow breaths before responding, and when he did he was careful to speak calmly. "It's frustrating. I helped my mother financially. I moved back in and took care of her, took her to her doctor's appointments, did most everything. I mean, I run my own business, I'm steady, responsible. These things..." He waved dismissively, "they happened decades ago. I was a teenager. And no one was hurt. And the breakdown—I was upset. I had a couple of bad nights, that's all. And now this."

"So it's unfair."

"It does sort of feel that way, yes."

"A misunderstanding, then?" Borgland had a pen ready to record Cyril's response.

"Sure," he said, smile rigid, "let's call it a misunderstanding."

Borgland nodded and then sat back in his swivel chair. "Well, we'll get to those things. But first I want some background, some context."

Cyril wondered how one trained for the job of probing another man's personality, weighing their experiences and actions, their opinions and dreams. It all seemed pretty ethereal. But Cyril went along with it, telling Mr. Bernard Borgland what he wanted to know about his childhood, his schooling, his work history, his interest in art. An hour later they parted amiably, with another handshake.

"I'd like to see some of your drawings," said Borgland.

"Sure," said Cyril.

On the drive home Cyril resolved not to go back. The worst that could happen was Borgland and Steve conferred, papers were filed, blah was blah'd, and Steve sold the house and cut Cyril a cheque. Bing, bang, boom. Whatever. He felt relieved.

At an intersection, he waited for an old couple to cross. They leaned forward as though hiking into a gale. Arm-in-arm they battled this wind, scarcely able to lift their feet. They may as well have been wearing lead boots their progress was so slow and torturous. The little green man turned into a red hand and yet they weren't even halfway across. They wore raincoats in spite of the heat, the old man wore a fedora, and his wife a checked scarf tied under her chin. Cyril's window was down, the heat hovering over the cars and the fumes parching his throat. Now they were in front of Cyril. The old man turned his head and managed a trembling gesture of apology for how far he had fallen from the grace of youth. Cyril raised his hand meaning it was fine, it was okay, there was no rush. The old man faced forward again and continued supporting his mate, the woman he'd known fifty, maybe sixty years, to the far side of this fierce river of hot, angry iron. The traffic light had gone from red to green to red again. Cyril watched the couple mount the kerb and then enjoy a moment—but only a moment—of relief before repositioning themselves for the next crosswalk. He thought of offering them a ride, but engines revved and the driver behind him honked and the light was green, so Cyril pressed the accelerator, certain that there was some meaning in this incident, yet unsure what it could be and how to find out except by drawing it. How did he draw the afternoon of the world, the waning day, the transient light as furtive as a deer in a parking lot puddled by rain? With his back to his mind and his face to the paper? Was that what Novak wanted?

Over the following week he devoted his energy to drawing. He felt good, he felt strong, and he felt right, he would participate in the show at The Arena. As for the psychiatric sessions, forget it, he was done. Yet on the morning that his second session with Borgland was scheduled Cyril found himself wide awake at five AM staring at the ceiling. He showered long, he shaved carefully, he paid particular attention to breakfast—16-grain toast with buckwheat honey, black coffee, and full-pulp orange juice—and then watched himself evaluate each drawing he was considering for the art show. When the time came for his appointment with Borgland—the appointment he was blowing off—he watched himself go to his closet and pick out his best shirt, brick coloured linen with slate buttons, a shirt he rarely got the opportunity to wear, then get in his van and follow the route out Kingsway toward Borgland's office. Halfway there he wrenched the wheel left and cut across the oncoming traffic—car horns warping past—down a side street and five minutes later was parking in front of Gilbert's apartment.

El Condor was scrolled across the glass door of the building in chipped bronze letters. A philodendron of prehistoric dimensions groped the windows as though frantic to escape. Cyril punched Gilbert's number, said, "Hey," the door buzzed and he swung it open. The carpeted corridor smelled of insecticide and attar of rose. He found Gilbert seated in front of the computer in a gold robe with indigo trim.

"My man, you're supposed to be on the couch."

Cyril stood on the Kashmiri carpet with peacocks and vines swirling about his feet. A puppy tumbled toward him and began wetly snuffling his shoes. Cyril backed up and the dog followed. It was small and blonde, with long ears and weepy eyes, and was apparently besotted by the smell of his feet.

"What do you think? Will Savannah like it?"

Cyril had no option but to succumb to the puppy's slobbery charm. He picked it up. Warm and soft and squirmy, it licked his face and he leaned away though couldn't keep from smiling.

"A lab?"

"A pure-bred lab, my friend."

Cyril held it to his chest. Pot-bellied and eager, with fur like cashmere. Gilbert had always had dogs as a kid, mutts that he tried training to attack but which could rarely overcome their amiable nature in spite of all his efforts to warp them into killers. Again the dog licked Cyril's throat with its slimy-soft tongue. Cyril poured the dog onto the floor where it stepped on its own ear and fell over. Thanks to the dog the mood had turned sweet, which screwed up everything, but he would not be diverted; he was here on a mission. "I saw you and Steve," he said louder than intended.

Gilbert did not interrupt his study of the stock market. "Saw me and Steve what?"

"Laughing."

"Laughing?" He shook his head as if at the absurdity of the very notion. "Where?"

"In front of his office. I was going by. You were laughing."

"And laughing is a problem?"

"Depends what you were laughing about."

Gilbert didn't hesitate, nor did he turn from the screen. "You."

Cyril watched Gilbert work the mouse. The screen was dense with tight columns of bold figures. Gilbert had always loved numbers, for in his mind they were the essence of money and measurement, and nothing was more important to measure than money. He should have gone into accounting like Paul. "This guy, Borgland, he's a real psychiatrist?"

"No."

Cyril waited for the punchline. Then he couldn't wait. "What do you mean?"

"I mean I never said he was a psychiatrist. I said he's a psy*chologist*. The difference being, my friend, that the former is a medical doctor, and the latter, ain't. *Capiche?* But for your purposes, my suspicious comrade, it's all the same. He can sign the paper and send you whistling on your merry way."

The dog curled up and with a great sigh went to sleep on the rug.

"So what's so funny about me?"

"You want a list? You spying for one thing." Gilbert spun his chair to face him. His eyes lacked their usual lustre, though they brightened noticing his shirt. "Nice." Gilbert's red robe was handmade by a tailor from Palermo on Commercial Drive. The couch was zebra, the coffee table smoked glass, the wall hung with framed prints of birds painted by Audubon. On another wall hung a row of framed photos of his daughters and granddaughters. Every one had inherited Gilbert's dense dark hair. The apartment's finery was all that remained from his various and uniformly disastrous marriages.

"I wasn't spying," said Cyril.

"Just getting a little paranoid maybe? I mean, I don't blame you, those two nephews of yours."

"I thought you hated Steve."

"Hate drains the energy. I'm all about unconditional love."

Cyril waited. Trading jabs was a waste of time. Silence was the only route through Gilbert's defences.

"I was visiting Steve for some legal counsel. Vis-à-vis reducing my debt load. I'm taking a pounding. The three harpies have me on the ropes."

"What happened to Murphy?"

"Murphy's on dialysis and a respirator."

The dog sat up then wobbled over to Gilbert who scooped it into his lap and stroked it under the chin. "You're tense, Cyril. I would be too. There's a lot at stake. But a word of advice: it reflects badly on you to go around making accusations. I mean, between me and you, okay, but be careful. People can spin that sort of thing. Don't go giving Stevie-boy any more ammo than he's already got." He checked his Rolex. "You're late."

In fact he pulled up in front of Borgland's right on time though he did not shut off the ignition or get out of the van, he sat there with the engine humming, battling a deeply rooted sense of obligation to go in and sit down and meekly undergo an interrogation with right and wrong answers, and serious consequences. Wasn't that the mature thing to do? Or was it the weak thing to do? Yet by law he was entitled to a portion of the estate, meaning that instead of full control of a five hundred thousand dollar house he'd get half or a third. But the principle, wasn't there a principle, wasn't there always a principle? He put the van in drive and headed home, singing.

FIVE

CYRIL SPENT THE morning of the art show wrapping his framed and glassed drawings in butcher paper for transport to The Arena. The gallery was on the street level of an old brick building that was deep and narrow, with a high ceiling and a fir slat floor. He arrived at noon to set up, thinking he was early, only to discover that the gallery was already so busy that the only wall space left was in the back by the toilet.

"You're by the crapper," said Richard. "That's good," he added, seeing Cyril's stricken face. "People will come out all relieved and yours'll be the first thing they'll see." Eyes wide behind his glasses, Richard retreated.

Cyril went back out to his van to get his drawings, fought the urge to simply drive away, and carried them back into the gallery. All around him clusters of people whispered, and snapped pictures and obsessed over their displays. He unwrapped his pieces then lined them against the wall wondering how to position them. The show was called *8 x 8: Eight works by eight artists.* Two rows of four would be boring. He considered two, four, two, or running them at an angle, or in an X. He shut his eyes and took a deep breath and reflected. Did he detect a hint of latrine in the air back here? Would that drive people away? Would they associate his stuff with excrement? Other artists drifted over for a look at his drawings, murmured approval then drifted away. He knew them from class, where there was always an atmosphere of camaraderie, yet now, in this new and public environment a competitive mood prevailed, and he re-evaluated his drawings: gravestones, 18 x 24 inches, black-metal-frames. In one, the stone was the back of a kneeling woman with a long and intricate braid, in another it was a burn barrel brimming with flames, in another it was a paint brush, bristles down, with an apple sporting a Stetson on top of the handle, in yet another the gravestone was a mirror with a winged horse ridden by a laughing demon reflected in the glass.

He went around looking at the other work and found Richard pricing his crabs at five hundred bucks apiece. Cyril hadn't priced his at all. Was his stuff worth what Richard's was? What if Richard sold out again and Cyril sold nothing? It was hard enough to do the drawings much less put them on display with a dollar figure beside them only to be ignored or ridiculed by self-styled experts who drifted in off the street for the free wine and cheese. Cyril returned to his corner and considered a price of three hundred dollars, or four, or two-fifty, or one. He shoved his hands in his pockets and inhaled a big breath— yes, definitely a hint of toilet. With a black pen he wrote $501 on the tags by each picture.

The opening didn't start until seven that evening. An eternity. He went home and cut and raked the lawn and pulled some weeds then went inside and vacuumed the hallway, dusted the Virgin Marys, took a damp Q-tip to the creases in the robe-work and the hair of the icon, and finally tried to do some drawing only to end up staring at his fingers. He gave up and listened to a phone message from John Boston offering him more money to take the job and if not could he recommend someone else. When you didn't want the work everyone wanted to give it to you. On the porch he looked for the cat but it was nowhere in sight.

He wandered the house and found himself at his mother's door. It had been almost two months since she'd died and he'd hardly glanced in. Pushing it open he saw, on the side table, his parents' wedding photo, black and white and grey with a few cream tones. His mother emanated an uncharacteristic optimism, her brow smooth, eyes calm, neck long in spite of the famine that had already eroded Ukraine like a flesh-eating disease. His father had slicked-back hair, a gaunt face, wary eyes, unable to forget, even on his wedding day, the thunder-heads of war. Cyril tried recalling the sound of his laughter and couldn't; the nearest his father ever came to joy was his quiet exultation the day Stalin had died.

Setting the photo on its doily, Cyril picked up the black velvet box and clicked it open. The gold bands were shiny on the inside and dull on the outside. He drew them from their slots and held them in his palm, fit the larger one onto his ring finger and the smaller, his mother's, onto his pinkie then extended his arm and gazed at his hand. What was the adage: all the fingers of the hand are not the same. Which finger was he? He removed the rings and returned them to their place and shut the box.

The oak bureau had three drawers and an oval mirror. Was there some message he was missing, some clue he was meant to discover? He looked behind the mirror, reached in under the drawers: nothing. Turning to the bed he hoisted the mattress. No, it was not a movie, it was his mother's bedroom, and there was no trap door or secret compartment, no shoe box full of letters, no revelatory photographs, no diary that explained all, whatever all was. Nonetheless, he opened the closet door. There were her clothes still on the hangers, the smell of old fabric, stale air and the leathery scent of six pairs of shoes set neatly side by side. He parted the clothes like curtains and found an old mirror leaning against the wall and himself reflected from the waist down. About to turn away he reached out and angled the mirror forward and found some large sheets of heavy-grade paper. In the kitchen he laid them on the table. Like ancient charts they wanted to curl in on themselves. He placed oranges on the corners to hold them down and discovered his long lost portfolio for art school, the Stalin-as-dervish postage stamps, including the unfinished one of Stalin on a swing. Thirty years stashed in the closet. His mother had not burned out the eyes. His first impression was favourable, odd, quirky, wobbly of execution, but interesting stuff. For the next half hour he looked at the pictures, wondering if they would have got him into art school, and if it would have made any difference in the long run?

He left the drawings where they were, and went into the living room, and clicked on the TV and caught the last bit of an episode of *I Spy*. How dated the clothes and cars, and leisurely the camera work. And there, pulling a gun on tennis-pro and CIA agent Kelly Robinson was a lithe Chinese woman in taut black leather: Connie. Cyril stepped close to the screen and stared. Yes, Connie.

Just keep walking Mr. Robinson

Where to, Miss... I didn't get your name.

Yevchenko.

Reaction shot on Robinson's shock and then bemusement.

My husband, she explains. And then adds, proudly, disdainfully, as if he, an American, could never hope to understand: I'm a communist. Turn here.

They enter a narrow twisting alley of overhanging balconies and strung laundry. Enigmatic Oriental faces peer from windows. A rickshaw squeezes past, knocking into them. Robinson ducks, spins, grips her wrist—the pistol falls and he catches it before it hits the ground. Advantage USA! He yanks her close. They stand chest to chest. He studies her; she glares her defiance. Will they kiss? He sneers, nostrils wide as if she bears the odour of Bolshevism. You're coming with me, Mrs. Yevchenko. But not so fast. She stomps his toe. He yelps and staggers. She snatches her gun and puts the barrel to the forehead of this Imperialist stooge.

What's your real name? he asks.

Flanagan. Her English suddenly flat and American. San Francisco. And with that she makes her escape into the labyrinthine alleys of the Forbidden City.

Cyril watched the episode to the end but Connie didn't show again.

He returned to the kitchen and considered two of the Stalin-as-dervishes.

As he was leaving with the two newly framed drawings, Cyril spotted the cat on a gravestone, his father's, a slab of black marble set flush to the ground. Stepping back into the kitchen he got the opera glasses and studied it: smoke-grey hair, a nick from one of its ears, looking supremely indifferent sitting there with such composed self-containment. Cyril poured cream into a saucer and set it on the porch then got going.

∽ ∾

A substantial woman of about sixty, straight sandy-grey hair stylishly cut at a slant, her lips a deep red, earrings white. Standing outside on the sidewalk looking through the gallery window, Cyril couldn't see much more, yet there was Novak parting the crowd like a ship and making a show of kissing the woman's hand. She pretended to slap his face. He pretended to be shocked. People laughed and applauded.

Gallery goers pushed past Cyril to get inside. He stepped back to protect the two framed drawings under his arm. It was warm. He was sweating. Head down, he plunged on in and headed straight for his corner, removed two graves, replaced them with the Stalins, and went back to his van. Had anyone even noticed? Returning minutes later, he went to the drinks table where a young woman in a white shirt and black bow tie was dispensing wine. Perhaps she saw the fear in his eyes because she filled his glass to the brim. Determined not to obsess over the attitudes of the people in front of his work, he turned in the opposite direction and began a circuit of the gallery. There was the woman who'd pretended to slap Novak in front of Richard's crabs, her head cocked as though looking through the lower half of bifocals.

Novak collared him. "Gravestones. Who would want to look at such things? Who would want to draw such things? Well-adjusted people are attracted to the sun, to the light. But artists are not well-adjusted. That's their strength. Don't do therapy. Don't untie your knots—tie them tighter!" His breath was acrid with wine and his hair a mess. "Very textural, these headstones of yours. The grass, the granite, the skin." He moved closer to Cyril's pictures and with his glass of red wine pointed at the nude-as-headstone. "I want to lick her spine. And that's good. I should want to lick her spine. Everyone who sees this picture should want to lick her spine. If you don't want to lick her spine you've failed."

"I'd lick her spine," said the woman who had mock-slapped Novak.

"Good." Novak wrapped his arm around Cyril's neck and growled, "Death. Defeat. Dirt. The Trinity."

"Are you going to introduce us?" she asked.

"Pamela Jean Preston, it is my great honour and privilege to present to you the one and only and all too humble Cyril Andrachuk."

They shook hands. Hers was cool; his was sweating.

"You don't like colour?" Preston asked, noting that Cyril's pictures were all in graphite.

"It's A-ok and okey-dokey and hunky-dory to listen to the grey voice," said Novak, whose English seemed to be growing loopier with every drink.

"Occasionally I venture into red," said Cyril.

"I've been shot in the fucking heart," observed Novak, who had missed his mouth with his glass and spilled wine down his white shirt. Cyril watched him go. Apparently Novak was so drunk he hadn't even noticed Cyril's late substitution of Stalins for gravestones.

Pamela asked, "Do you have a death obsession?"

"I grew up across from a cemetery."

"Was that depressing?"

"I'm not sure. It's just what it was."

"My father owned a cemetery. Or was the director. One or the other. Maybe both." Plucked eyebrows coming together, she frowned in a moment of genuine confusion. "He owned so much it's hard to keep track."

Cyril knew of her. Eldest daughter of Jerry Preston, evangelical millionaire who had made his fortune in used cars and billboards. "Was that depressing?"

"Hell, no. I had everything. Horses, holidays. You name it." She wore a dress of crinkly black fabric that hugged her fulsome figure, an ivory locket in the form of a heart, white bracelets, and carried a small cream purse. "Is this your first showing?" she asked.

Cyril lied and nodded.

She placed her palm flat to his chest as if to calm his heart and said, "Relax. Breathe."

He breathed. She smelled like gin and milk.

Winking, she said, "Try to enjoy yourself," and glided away.

He felt curiously relieved, as though having been blessed by a minor saint.

As Pamela slid off through the crowd, Cyril noted two other women, older, in their seventies, perambulating the gallery arm-in-arm, heads tilted as though to share scandal. They were elegant and animated, the very opposite of his mother. She should be here. Gloom draped him. The image of her corpse in the coffin in the ground drove itself like a stake into his heart. Novak passed carrying two glasses sloshing with wine, sipping alternately from one then the other. A cluster of people gathered in front of Cyril's work and he gave in to deciphering their body language. Mocking? Mild interest? Genuine fascination? They wheeled away, laughing. Was it sneering laughter or delighted laughter? One had rolled their eyes, he was sure of it. He raised his glass but it was empty. He got a refill and held it like a protective crucifix.

The crowd parted long enough for Cyril to spot Richard accepting a business card from one of the elderly matrons who had been touring the room. A kid in a Mohawk passed Cyril's picture, belching as he entered the washroom; when he came back out he made a great performance of yawning. Cyril went to the washroom himself and splashed cold water on his face. Leaning on the sink he stared at himself: five hundred and one dollars. Was he mad?

When he emerged he stood to one side watching the crowd. Half recognized faces spun past, but one snagged his attention like a burr. *Was it? It was.* Cyril couldn't remember the man's name but knew his face, older, greyer, fatter, but definitely the nasty one from his art school interview all those years ago. The guy carried his head high and kept his mouth shut as though holding his breath against a rising stench. Hands clasped behind his back and chin out like the prow of a royal yacht, he sailed through the crowd and hove to before Cyril's work. His eyebrows jumped in what appeared to be alarm, went down in what appeared to be disapproval, then his lips pooched out as he exercised patience, stretched wide in skepticism, and finally he flinched as though grit had been spat into his eyes. He looked around in horror. Had he recognized the Stalins? Was he searching for the scurrilous Cyril who had managed to sneak past him? Was he about to complain? Wheeling to his right he launched himself toward the toilet as though to be sick. As far as Cyril could tell he never emerged.

Novak was singing in a surprisingly melodious baritone while Richard was on his knees before Pamela as if proposing marriage. Pamela's head dropped back and her laughter gushed like a bouquet of yellow flowers. Cyril drank more wine. Now one of the matrons who had given Richard her card was writing him a cheque and Pamela was putting a red sticker beside one of the crabs. There was a sparkling fountain of laughter and congratulations. Novak joined in, clapping Richard on the back and clinking his glass.

Cyril looked at the door. How clear and cool the air would be outside. He discovered that his glass was empty yet again and that his head hurt. As he moved toward the bar Pamela caught his elbow and turned him back in the other direction. They stopped before his drawings.

"I don't know about those Stalins," she said, "but I do like the others." She compressed her lips and nodded once, as if reconfirming this strange but undeniable fact. Her white clip-on earrings were ivory—Cyril could see the grain—and they were carved in the shape of tiny ears. "I especially like this one." She pointed to the woman with the braid down her naked back. Cyril tried seeing it through Pamela's eyes. Her eyes, he noted, were heavily veined, as if with incandescent filaments. "Yes," she said again, "I like it."

Cyril heard himself ask, "Why?"

She turned and regarded him with a bewildered and yet bemused smile. She sucked her teeth. She turned back to the picture. For a full minute they stood side-by-side staring at the woman's naked back and long braid. Finally she shrugged. "Like I said, I don't know. I just do."

"Thank you," said Cyril.

"No, no. Thank *you.*" She placed her hand on his forearm. "Wait here."

Cyril watched her go off through the crowd and then return a moment later holding something between her thumb and forefinger. She held it up as though it was a gem. "I want it— you *will* sell it to me?"

"Of course!"

"Good." She put a red sticker by the picture. "Congratulations," she said. "To both of us."

Cyril felt as if he'd just lost his virginity.

"Breathe," she reminded him, then smiled again, one corner of her mouth curling upward. "Oh." She opened her bag and found her chequebook. "I suppose I owe you money." She wrote his name and five hundred "and one dollars," she said aloud, and slipped it into his shirt pocket and gave it a tap. "Keep the commission."

Seeing what was under way, Novak and Richard joined them along with others.

"I've just bought a work of art," announced Pamela.

There were murmurs of approval and renewed interest in Cyril's pictures. Novak gripped him by the back of the neck and gave it a hearty squeeze. Richard slipped away. The gallery was now packed, the air simultaneously sour and fragrant with perfume and bodies. Cheque in his pocket, red sticker by his drawing—by his *work*—an elated Cyril floated toward the bar to treat himself to another glass of wine and tried not to smile too widely.

SIX

CYRIL SLEPT LATE and when he went onto the porch with his coffee, discovered that the saucer was empty. He scanned the cemetery with the opera glasses but there was no cat. It was Monday morning and the city was at work. He felt no guilt. As he trained the opera glasses on his mother's grave he only wished she could have been at the show last night. In the end he'd sold three pictures: two gravestones, one Stalin. Three sales; fifteen hundred and three dollars. He could have danced. In fact he had danced when he got home last night. That Richard had also sold three in no way diminished his sense of triumph.

Gilbert hadn't shown, which was curious because it was just the sort of event he thrived upon, a combination of new people, new contacts, and free liquor. He'd have been all over Pamela, having long been an admirer of her father's business smarts.

Cyril refilled the saucer then returned to the gallery to take down his pictures. Empty wine glasses sat on ledges and in corners. There was a bow tie and, bizarrely, a pair of grey slacks. Pamela was there with Novak and a few others. Pamela wore embroidered kung fu slippers, baggy black pants with ties at the ankles and waist, an Oriental jacket with gold stitching. When she saw Cyril she left Novak and caught Cyril's face in her hands and air-kissed him once, twice, and the third time square on the mouth. Her hands were cold but her eyes radiant. She gripped his elbow and they proceeded to perambulate the gallery apart from the others.

"You have arrived," she said. "You must consider your future, your career, and have a show of your own."

Cyril nodded bravely. "Right."

She tightened her hold on him.

"Get a room," called Novak.

Pamela said in a voice loud enough for Novak to hear: "A disgusting creature. We should get him deported." As they continued their perambulation she became reflective. "You're at a good age for an artist." Her voice rose another notch, "unlike some people. Old enough to be mature but not so old as to be old."

Cyril nodded as if he'd been thinking the same thing. Was she offering him his own show? Before he could ask her, Richard arrived looking severely hungover in ragged jeans and torn T-shirt. Pamela gave Cyril's elbow one last squeeze, reminded him to breathe, and sailed off to capture Richard. Gripping one of Richard's biceps, she growled. "Nice arms, kiddo."

When Cyril got home the saucer was empty and the cat crouched in the corner of the yard, regarding him from the safety of the thorny yellow roses. He got his pad and did a few sketches.

He spent the next morning in Steve's office going over the psychologist's report. According to Borgland, Cyril was a man capable of caring and reflection and sensitivity, with a deep sense of justice and injustice. He was also angry and conflicted and prone to violent, impulsive behaviour that could result in harm to himself and to others, as well as lead to financial ruin. Thirteen pages of single-spaced text was summarized under a subtitle: Conclusions and Recommendations. *It is best for all concerned that control of the estate be given over to Steven George Andrachuk.*

"All that from one session?"

"You bailed," said Steve. "I mean in some ways I can't blame you. Not exactly fun getting grilled like that."

Cyril considered his nephew, trying to gauge his level of sincerity. Ever since the conditions of the will had been revealed, Cyril had been thinking about what the house meant to him, trying to measure his degree of attachment to it, the way someone might attribute significance to an heirloom or a piece of land. His father had not built the house, but he had done extensive repairs, and Cyril had spent his childhood there, it was the site of memories, such as his parents dancing one New Year's, not Ukrainian New Year but December thirty-first, the shouts and horns blaring up and down the street, Cyril banging a wooden spoon on a pan, Paul lighting firecrackers on the porch. That would have been about 1950, the only time Cyril could ever recall his parents dancing. Still, it was just a house, one of dozens of identical boxes on the same street, a heap of aging wood.

"The only thing to do is carry on," Steve continued, "and the best way to carry on—for all of us—is by placing a reverse mortgage on the house." He began explaining the details but Cyril interrupted saying that he knew what a reverse mortgage was.

"So there are no questions?"

"Seems clear enough," said Cyril.

"Right." Steve became brisk. There were documents to sign. He reassured Cyril that there was nothing to worry about, that it would be business as usual. "You're the *de facto* if not legal owner of the house."

Cyril nodded. *De facto* meant *de fucto* all.

"It's your home."

Again Cyril nodded. Steve had got what he wanted; he wouldn't get Cyril's blessing too.

Steve stapled papers together, folded them, slid them into an envelope, slid the envelope across the desk then mustered the courage to look directly at Cyril, compressing his lips and shrugging in a show of innocence. Cyril maintained a neutral expression. Steve stood and extended his hand, the final formality. Cyril stood and shook Steve's hand and accepted the manila envelope, at which Steve risked a smile and made a move to come around the desk and escort Cyril out. But Cyril sat back down. Steve halted. His eyebrows jumped. Uncle Cyril, it seemed, was about to fuck things up. He exhaled long and made a show of glancing at his watch, meaning he was a busy man. "Something else?"

Cyril settled back into the chair, the padding sighing beneath him, crossed his legs and folded his hands on top of the envelope in his lap. He gazed past Steve out the window at the apartment building across the alley. It needed paint. "I won't stay long. Don't worry."

"Oh. No. Hey." Steve returned to his seat and prepared to be a good listener.

Cyril said, "Your grandmother and I had a tense relationship. We had issues. We blamed each other for things. But one thing I'm not to blame for is your dad's death."

"Cyril."

"Your dad and I did not get along."

"I know."

"I'm sure you do. But I can't help having been born in 1945 instead of 1937. I offered my kidney. I was willing to give him one. I signed the papers."

Steve's face tightened. "He sensed reluctance." He spoke as if his jaw was wired shut.

"Of course he did. Because I was reluctant. I signed the papers, though. I made the decision. I took the step. But here's the question: did you offer one of yours?"

Steve's head jerked back as if Cyril had swung at him.

"I don't recall you or your brother offering any help."

"He already told us not to. He said don't even think about it."

"But it was alright for me?"

"I don't know."

"You don't know? You knew enough to blame me."

Steve slammed both of his palms down on the desk. "What do you want me to say?"

Cyril spoke quietly, almost reflectively, because the realization had been so slow in surfacing. "Steve, it doesn't matter what you say. It doesn't matter what you think. What matters is what I think. And I'm not to blame. I thought I was. For years I accepted that I was. But that's wrong. I. Am. Not. To. Blame. And if you and your grandmother wanted to think otherwise, if you still want to keep punishing me then do your worst. I mean, you already have." He held up the envelope, then sailed it into Steve's chest. At the door he turned and asked, "Oh. One more thing. And be honest for once. Was Gilbert in on this?"

Steve looked at Cyril from under the brow of his lowered head and nodded. Then he recovered. He sat back and set his palms flat on the desk because now it was his turn. "They didn't exclude you. It had nothing to do with you. They just wanted to put it all behind them. It was the only way they could cope. She told me."

"She seems to have told you a lot of things."

Steve looked genuinely helpless. "Maybe because by then it didn't matter."

The words reverberated through Cyril's mind as he drove home. His parents had been given interior lives with complex pasts that stretched into earliest childhoods that were unique to them and them alone. He'd always known this—only now he knew it better.

When he got home, he found the saucer empty and the cat in the roses. Cyril opened a tin of salmon and forked some into the saucer, and that evening as the sky was turning a dusty pink and crows were racketing in the cemetery, he sat in the kitchen nook watching the cat creep up onto the porch. He sketched the cat as it ate the salmon. When it was done it spent a full ten minutes grooming, going over its paws, its stomach, its tail, curling around and doing its back. Cyril did a dozen sketches, working fast though sure to turn the pages slowly so as not to startle it.

SEVEN

THE KNOCK ON the door sounded like the rattle of ancient plumbing. Cyril looked at the pair of pipes in the corner that ran from the ceiling down through the floor. An inch in diameter, they'd been repainted so many times they resembled melting candles, and regularly shuddered as if choking. The knock came again. No, not the pipes. One of the other tenants hitting him up for dough? Cyril had got a hundred and sixty thousand dollars six months ago when Steve had sold the house. Cyril's new neighbours had smelled money, and when they came knocking he'd been free with the twenty dollar bills and consequently become a great favourite. Gilbert had visited once. Cyril had said little as his old friend babbled excuses about being desperately broke due to alimony, the stock market, and the fact that no one took cabs anymore.

"How much did Steve give you?"

Gilbert looked away, unable to meet Cyril's eyes. "Ten grand."

Cyril had asked about Savannah, and Gilbert said grandpa had become invisible. That was sad but in Cyril's experience invisibility was not without its liberating aspect. Gilbert sat with his head in his hands and cried, though whether due to Savannah's indifference or because he'd scammed Cyril, or both, was not clear. Placing his hand on Gilbert's shoulder he'd gently signalled that it was time to go. Cyril had said he'd give him a call. So far he hadn't. He'd been busy, spending all his time drawing and in the Fine Arts Department of the new library that was shaped like the Roman Coliseum.

The knock came again. He lay down his pencil and closed the sketchbook and looked at the door. Crossing the room—a journey of five steps—he opened up and found Connie standing there in the corridor. She wore blue jeans and a red pullover, her hair pinned in a loose heap atop her head, over her shoulder a black, cotton bag decorated with bits of coloured glass.

He didn't miss a beat. "About time."

"Traffic was bad."

"The important thing is you're here."

She studied him with cautious delight.

"Good to see you," he said.

Her voice softened. "You too." She peered in at the room then at the number on the door. "Cyril, is this..."

"Yup."

"Is he—" She pointed toward the office at the end of the corridor.

"His son."

"Did you plan this?"

"I was just looking for a cheap place for a week or two, then a week or two became a month or two, and then, well..."

They embraced. He held her close, squeezing until she sighed and then he squeezed her more. She smelled good, so good. It occurred to him that he could be humiliated at being found here. It also occurred to him that he wasn't.

"I've been thinking about you," she said, cheek against his chest and arms around his waist.

He felt the vibration of her voice in his breastbone. He didn't say how often he'd thought of her. "That's good to hear." He hoped he didn't come across as desolate. He didn't feel desolate, in fact he felt pretty good. He had a show coming up at The Arena.

When they stood back they held on to each other's hands. Her fingers were warm and fine. She was no longer wearing all those silver rings.

"Gilbert told me what happened."

Cyril nodded and wondered what he hadn't told her. "I'm sure his version is interesting."

"Got into a cab and there he was," she said. "Fatter, but just the same."

"Come on in."

Connie advanced tentatively into the room, gazing around as though entering a cave gleaming with rare mineral formations. Cyril fetched the wooden chair from the table and set it down for her. She put one hand on the chair but was diverted by the drawings. Every inch of wall as high as Cyril could reach was covered with his work. Connie studied them like an explorer, peering closely then stepping back, turning, discovering another here, another there, moving left, moving right, as though venturing deeper into a maze. There were studies of street people forlorn against walls or laughing in groups. Two drinkers at a terry cloth-covered pub table, each gazing in their own direction, each with a hand on a beer glass detailed right down to the lacework of foam beneath the plimsoll line. A group doing tai chi in a park. A crate of cabbages. A crumpled Coke can, dilapidated Victorian houses, a series of shovels and sunflowers, the shovels standing blade up, dark counterpoint to the radiant blooms.

"This is—"

"Crazy?"

"I was going to say intense. You really live here. I mean, I was only playing a part…"

Cyril considered that. "You're not the only one who sees the place and gets worried."

He described how one afternoon Novak had arrived with Pamela Jean Preston and while both had nodded approvingly at the work, Pamela seemed worried. She'd gripped Cyril's face with both hands and staring sternly into his eyes warned him, "Don't swim too far from the ship. Don't go drowning on us."

"If you do, do it quick," Novak had said.

Pamela had glared him into silence.

Now Connie discovered a framed drawing of a grey cat sleeping on a gravestone. Curled, neat, relaxed, yet alert. The drawing sat on the side-table, flanked by sticks of smouldering incense protruding from miniature iron cauldrons filled with sand. Beside it was a bowl of oranges. "You're a cat worshiper?"

"He lives in the cemetery. I feed him."

Connie remembered the cemetery. "The cemeteries in LA are lousy," she said. "The weather's too good. Too much sun. Cemeteries lose something in sunshine. They need rain and shade. Gloom." She sat on the wooden chair, gaze returning to Cyril every few seconds as if to be sure it was really him.

She studied a drawing of a laughing boy on a swing. He was about three years old. Up high, at the top of the swing's arc, he'd been thrown free of the seat and launched into the air toward the outstretched arms of a man waiting in the bottom left corner. The drawing was bold, the boy's body had weight, the lines of his legs single strokes from hip to heel, the laces of his runners flying loose. His fists were free of the chain that held the seat and his eyes were closed—as were the eyes of the laughing man waiting with his arms outstretched to catch him. Each seemed to possess faith in the other. Connie studied the drawing for a long time, turning it this way and that as though a different angle might reveal more.

She gestured around the room as though at the miracle of the constellations. "You see things," she said.

"Yeah. They tried saying I'm delusional."

"Who?"

Cyril didn't want to get into it. He no longer obsessed over the will. Gesturing vaguely over his shoulder, he said, "Them."

"Fuck Them. Delusions are good. I meant you see things in things. Thingyness. Like that orange. It's not just any orange. It's *that* orange. It's got a history, a personality. You could interview that orange and it would tell you about its life, whether it was a happy or sad orange. It could describe its position in the tree: which branch, how high, the view, the sun's heat on its peel, the seeds growing inside it, its cute little navel swelling until it became an outie. Then there's the birds. The robins and crows—those damn crows and their damn cawing!" She pressed her palms to her ears as if the racket was driving her mad. She crossed her arms over her chest and became small, her voice grave. "And of course all its friends. The ones that had so much hope, the ones that fell before their time, the ones that lay there on the ground waiting for the worms..."

Cyril applauded.

∽∾ ∽∾

They walked past a school and a field and sat at a table outside a bakery and convenience store. It was a quiet street but only half a block away traffic clamoured like a river of metal while late afternoon sun spoked through the maples. It had rained all morning then cleared and now the street gave off the froggy smell of mulch and pavement. It was May, and there were robins and squirrels in the wide-leafed trees. Connie settled deep in her plastic chair and stretched out her legs and crossed them at the ankles and described her role in the film that had brought her to town.

"It's about this big," she said, holding her thumb and fore-finger a centimetre apart. "Three scenes, thirteen lines. I play a vengeful wife. So I bring a lot of experience to the role."

Cyril didn't want to hear about her marriages.

She grew solemn. "I've actually been planning on moving back here. Been thinking about it a long time. Need to get some balance. I've spent so long chasing the mirage I don't know what's real and what isn't. Cameras are dangerous that way. They do things. They whisper. And they're very hard to resist."

Someone was playing a saxophone down the street and Cyril began describing his dream of them in the jazz club, and she said she often dreamed of them in that tree in the cemetery.

They agreed that it was a good tree, a great tree, and that they should go and visit it.

The afternoon light illuminated the wet maples. Connie said she missed the rain. "Never thought I'd say that. But all that dry air gives you a sore throat and too much sun blinds you. It's shrill. Makes your eyes deaf. Grey's good sometimes. A very underrated colour," she added. Then, hearing herself, she grew shy. "So say I to you."

Cyril agreed that grey got a bad rap. "It has the widest spectrum, goes all the way from white to black. I used to think the soul was grey."

"And now?"

"I don't know. I think maybe it changes colour."

∽ ∾

They paused where vendors had set out books, tapes, LPs and jewelry on the sidewalk. Connie admired a pair of gold hoop earrings, vacillating as to whether to buy, in the end putting them back in the lid of the shoebox where they were displayed. When she moved on to peruse some scarves, Cyril quickly purchased the earrings and slipped them into his pocket.

∽ ∾

"The bed used to be like a hammock."

"I put a sheet of plywood under the mattress."

"You always had a practical side." He was not sure he agreed, but was curious that she seemed to think so. She settled in closer and pulled the blanket up. "How long you plan on staying here?"

"What, you don't like it?"

"I love it. It's all I've ever dreamed of. Especially the pigeons on the windowsill and the way the pipes wobble. It's just that you're kind of running out of room. Or do you plan on renting the one next door too and knocking out the wall?"

"That's not a bad idea," he said, meaning it. "You serious about moving back?" He tried not to sound too hopeful yet not too offhand.

She took an orange from a bowl beside the bed, examined it then put it back. "Yeah. Why not?" There was an edge to her voice, as if she'd been over this before. "It's not a defeat. There's lots of stuff going on up here. More than ever." Then she dropped the defiance and, as if confessing said, "I'm fifty."

Cyril sucked air in shock; she made a fist as though to punch him. He caught her hand and kissed it. There was a hint of citrus.

"It's just that you wonder what you've achieved," she said.

"I'll tell you what you've achieved: you haven't spent thirty years wishing you'd done something else."

Her gaze searched him. She shifted closer. Their legs were entwined, her skin hot. Cyril had forgotten how reassuring physical contact was. Resting his arm on her thigh he stroked it languidly and they kissed for a while and she said again how often she thought of him, and then she fell asleep. Her breathing settled into a deep slow rhythm. He studied her then shut his eyes as well but couldn't drift off. A bottle burst in the alley, then came the clatter of a shopping cart, followed by a siren and, just outside the window, the clapping of a frightened pigeon. He sat up and swung his legs out of the bed.

Connie woke. "Cyril?"

"I don't know," he said.

"Don't know what?"

"I've been pissed off at you ever since that movie. You should have come back out. We could've gone to something else. Together."

She curled on her side and after a while said, "You're right. I thought about it. I almost cashed in my ticket and came back out. I'm sorry. I was seventeen. Selfish. Kind of still am."

Cyril pressed his palms down on the bed as if about to stand.

Connie put her hand on his back as if to hold him. "Draw me."

"When?"

"Now."

She handed him the drawing book from the side table.

"Takes time."

"I've got time."

"You're leaving."

"I'm coming back."

"Are you?"

"Yes."

He considered that. "I work slowly."

"What, you think I want some half-assed job? Some sketch? Wham-bam-thank-you-ma'am?"

He studied her in the candle light, his eye tracing the contours of her face, its light and shadow, the shape of her mouth and nose, the lengths of her eyes, the curl of her ear. She was wearing the hoop earrings he'd bought her.

After a moment she asked, "Is this how it begins?"

He shrugged. "It could be."

ABOUT THE AUTHOR

Grant Buday has published nine books and many articles, essays, and short stories in Canadian magazines and quarterlies. While he has travelled extensively throughout the world he currently lives on Mayne Island, British Columbia, with his wife and son, where he manages a recycling depot.

ACKNOWLEDGMENTS

I want to thank Paul Bondarenko for his Ukrainian language lessons, and all the people I strong-armed into reading, and rereading, this manuscript: the herr doktor Simon Hearn, Yasuko Thanh, Joy Gugeler, Jack Schofield, and most especially Eden.